"When do we start doing this for real?"

"Tomorrow."

"Do I get to keep my clothes on?" Jarod asked cheekily with a naughty sparkle in his eyes. Lacey fumbled the camera.

"Depends on whether you mean during or after the shoot," she said off the cuff, shocking herself—it was something the "old" her would have said without a second thought, and she couldn't stop a smile as she watched his shocked reaction.

Score one for Lacey. She could still come out and play, apparently.

He didn't say anything else, and she finished the last roll of film, pleased with herself for the shots and for finding a little of her own spark. Temptation quelled doubt for the moment.

Lieutenant Wyatt had something special, a mysterious quality that reached past her fears and made her see what she'd been missing out on for some time. This tall Texas cop might be good for her, after all.

Did she dare?

Dear Reader,

Writing about heroes is always fun—who doesn't like thinking about hot guys all day? However, my heroine, Lacey Graham, is a woman who really doesn't believe in heroes anymore, and I wanted to find the perfect guy to show her they are still out there.

Texas Ranger Lieutenant Jarod Wyatt appeared, and is definitely the man to make Lacey believe again. Jarod is a good man, and so very, very sexy. I loved the way these two characters played, worked and grew together on the pages, dealing with their problems while falling in love, even though neither expected it.

Another theme in this book is how important it is for women to talk and share with each other. Sometimes it's just to blow off steam, and other times it can be lifesaving to share what we know and feel. We do that through romance novels, on message boards on the Internet and over lunch with our friends. It's important.

Go hug your hero, and then sit and read this book. I hope you enjoy it. Share it with your friends. Feel free to drop me an e-mail or stop by my blog at www.loveisanexplodingcigar.com to chat and let me know what you think. I'd love to hear from you.

Sincerely,

Samantha Hunter

Hard To Resist

SAMANTHA HUNTER

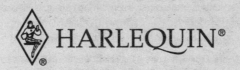

TORONTO • NEW YORK • LONDON
AMSTERDAM • PARIS • SYDNEY • HAMBURG
STOCKHOLM • ATHENS • TOKYO • MILAN • MADRID
PRAGUE • WARSAW • BUDAPEST • AUCKLAND

Recycling programs
for this product may
not exist in your area.

ISBN-13: 978-0-373-79482-9

HARD TO RESIST

Copyright © 2009 by Samantha Hunter.

ABOUT THE AUTHOR

Samantha Hunter lives in Syracuse, New York, where she writes full-time for Harlequin Books. When she's not plotting her next story, Sam likes to work in her garden, quilt, cook, read and spend time with her husband and their dogs. Most days you can find Sam chatting on the Harlequin Blaze boards at eHarlequin.com, or you can check out what's new, enter contests, or drop her a note at her Web site, www.samanthahunter.com.

Books by Samantha Hunter

Don't miss any of our special offers. Write to us at the following address for information on our newest releases.

Harlequin Reader Service
U.S.: 3010 Walden Ave., P.O. Box 1325, Buffalo, NY 14269
Canadian: P.O. Box 609, Fort Erie, Ont. L2A 5X3

For all my friends at Love Is an Exploding Cigar, who make every day, even tough writing days, fun.

1

"I THINK WE REALLY might have found the twelve sexiest men in America," Lacey Graham's assistant, Jackie, sighed as they took in the photographic buffet of gorgeous men before them on the project board. The final selections for the "Sexiest American Heroes" calendar had been made the week before. As photographer for the project, these gorgeous guys were all now in Lacey's capable hands.

Lacey stood back, one arm wrapped across her middle with her other elbow balancing on it, her chin resting in her fingers as she assessed the blowups of the hunks with a cool, experienced eye.

Too many blondes in a row in March, April and May—she'd switch April with August. Since they were in October now, she'd reversed the schedule, starting with Mr. December, who was set to arrive tomorrow, and November a few days later. She wanted to take them one at a time, calling them back at a later date for group cover shots.

She and Jackie had been juggling these promo shots all day, most of which were not professionally done but were good enough for roughs. Actually, it was impressive how incredible these men looked in the bad lighting and overly bright PR poses. Her hands itched to get to work, to get them in the right setting, good light.

"I don't think I've ever seen such a collection of perfect men all in one place." Jackie sighed. "I want them all, and not necessarily one at a time."

Lacey chuckled. "Down, girl. Don't you have a steady boyfriend?"

"Well, sure, but I can window-shop, can't I? K.C. is my guy, and he knows it, but frankly, he's not above checking out some beautiful woman when she walks by and turnaround is fair play. So if you had to choose…?" Jackie prompted Lacey mischievously.

Lacey shook her head, not interested. She looked at the men on the board in the only way she could, as professional modeling subjects and that was all. She rubbed her right forearm, knowing it was healed, but a shadow of an ache lingered anyway. Her last lover had not taken her attempts to break up very well, leaving her with a broken forearm as a parting gift, along with an assortment of bruises and a nasty laceration that had taken several stitches. Broken hearts were something you could get over most of the time, but having someone break your arm wasn't easily forgotten.

Swallowing deeply, she studied the board, fighting the sick feeling in her stomach that she got whenever she thought about being with a man. It would pass. She'd get back in the game at some point. When *she* was ready and not before, not even for guys like the ones lined up in front of her. Until then, she'd keep to herself and focus on her work. That was what mattered.

No one here knew her secret.

Jackie didn't know and no one was going to know about what had happened with Scott, her ex. On the advice of the doctor who treated her arm, Lacey had made one visit to an abuse counselor when she'd arrived in the city. Once she saw the haunted expressions of the women sitting in the lobby, she'd walked back out. That wasn't her. She'd handle it on her own.

What Scott had done to her had been a onetime thing, a huge, incredibly stupid mistake. But Lacey hadn't waited around for more and wouldn't allow it to happen again. She wasn't like the women who were trapped or who wouldn't leave.

Still, the memory pinched at her as much as the residual ache in her arm. On a certain level, she was irritated with herself for not being able to enjoy the beauty of the men as she once would have done. Like Jackie said, there was nothing wrong with looking.

There was no doubt that the array of males she'd be working with were prime fantasy material. She also knew she shouldn't change her perception of all men because of one bad apple. She *knew* that—in her head.

Her heart, however, was still playing "keep away," and so was her body. She'd made a few small forays into a normal dating life—tried to go out to clubs with friends—but it hadn't worked out. The thought of a man touching her, even to dance…well…not yet.

"I'm a professional. I don't have a favorite," she said primly, breaking the spell of her thoughts.

Jackie wasn't buying it. "Ha. Give me a break. Check

out Mr. November and tell me he's not absolutely perfect."

Lacey glanced up, relenting just slightly. "No one is perfect."

"Cynic."

"Groupie."

They grinned at each other, and Lacey relented a little. "It is hard to resist an honest-to-goodness cowboy."

"Not a cowboy, a Texas Ranger," Jackie corrected with flourish. "Rough, rugged, and they always get their man."

"Isn't that the Mounties?"

"Whatever. I bet they always get their girl, too."

Lacey studied the man staring out from the Ranger's PR photo and smiled. "He's got good eyes. Dark hair, dark eyes. That straight jawline could be on a statue at the Met, but he's so serious. All the rest are smiling."

"Maybe he doesn't like having his picture taken."

"We'll have to change that right quick," Lacey said in a mock Western accent, slipping out of her serious self for a moment, though she couldn't joke about the facts in front of her.

"This guy is the real deal. Look at his bio. Very single, career cop, has more awards and recognitions than I can count. He was nominated for the calendar by his community after he stopped a school shooter single-handedly. He found the guy targeting a local migrant school before the shooting happened. Tracked him through the Texas desert for five days and brought him back. Alive."

"Wow," Jackie breathed the word, fanning her face, and Lacey had to agree. *Wow* indeed.

Lacey couldn't help but be impressed with the stories of the twelve men on her wall. They were good men. Men who put their lives on the line to help others. The one thing all of the calendar candidates had in common was that they'd pitched in to help during the weeks of 9/11, one of the criteria for the application.

The *Bliss* calendar this year was going to be a smash, a celebration of the best of the best. It was also going to be a very visible leap for Lacey into the world of commercial photography. It could push her to the top. That was what she was counting on, anyway.

Lacey had given up several other opportunities to land the deal. The women's magazine equivalent of the *Sports Illustrated Swimsuit Issue,* the *Bliss* project was the chance of a lifetime.

She wasn't going to let the past get the best of her.

Eyeing Mr. November again, she allowed herself to imagine the possibilities, just for a second.

"His eyes *are* good," Jackie agreed, "but I can't wait to see him with his shirt off. I bet he has great abs, naturally defined, not gym-machine generated."

Lacey agreed. "I love the slope of the croup…"

"The…*what?*" Jackie frowned at her as if she was nuts.

Lacey laughed. "Sorry. My parents raised horses back in Nevada, and sometimes I can't help thinking about people's bodies in equine terms. Especially men."

"I'll bet he's hung like a—"

"Jackie!" Lacey admonished, laughing. "We're not taking *those* kinds of pictures."

"Hey, gotta show some skin for *Bliss*. But what's the slope of the— What was it again?"

"Croup. On a horse, it's the curve that follows the hip to the tip of the tail—right about here on our handsome model," she said, leaning in to trace the masculine line from hip over his hindquarters.

"Oh. Yeah. I *love* that part," Jackie said approvingly. "Very important for good thrust, yes?"

Lacey choked on a shocked laugh, pulling her hand back as she realized she hadn't withdrawn her finger from the photograph yet, her cheeks catching fire. Maybe she wasn't quite as detached as she thought she was.

"Yes, I suppose it would be. Thanks for the visual. I guess Mr. December should be here tomorrow, right?"

Jackie snapped to attention. "Oh, crap, I meant to tell you—I had to change up the first two appointments. November is coming in first because December's wife went into labor, so he won't be in for a week or so."

"Oh, well, good for them. We should send something, congratulations, flowers, whatever," Lacey commented absently, still studying the pictures.

"Already done."

"You're the best."

"So, Mr. Luscious should be arriving at LaGuardia around 10:00 a.m.—I'll meet him, of course." Jackie grinned like a cat swallowing a whole flock of canaries. "And then after lunch you'll meet him for an afternoon planning session, some studio time, and get out on the shoot day after tomorrow. He's single. No babies to worry about, thank the heavens."

"Sounds good. Thanks so much for all of your help. I've never had a full-time assistant before. I could get used to it."

"Hit a bull's-eye with this job, and you'll need one to keep up with all the projects that will be coming your way," Jackie said sincerely, patting Lacey's arm. "Uh, I have to go. I'm meeting Kenny at the rib place he's been insisting on going to. You want to come along? He's into photography, too, and was hoping to talk shop with you at some point."

"Really? I didn't know that—what's he do?"

Jackie shrugged. "He's been doing all kinds of things for a while. He had a small gallery show, and he's been picking up some brochure work, catalogs, that kind of thing."

"Everyone has to start somewhere."

"He's really good—I could show you some of his stuff sometime."

Lacey smiled, but always felt awkward in situations where up-and-coming photographers wanted to make contact, but it was how the game was played, and Jackie was her assistant.

"Sure—but you go ahead for dinner. I have work to finish up here. Thanks, though."

"Okay, I'll have your hunk here for you safe and sound tomorrow."

"Don't take a bite out of him before you get here."

Jackie stuck her tongue out. "Spoilsport."

Lacey grinned, then was left alone to quietly study

the men. They were all amazing, although Jackie was right. November stood out. Maybe slightly older than the others, he had more presence, more…*something*. Manliness, charisma… Those steady brown eyes might have been staring down a suspect as much as a camera as he peered out from the picture. *Dangerous*. Not to be messed with.

Would he look at her that way? Did his eyes soften when he was with a lover? Naked, tangled in silky sheets, skin to skin? Was he still all hard edges and intense eyes then?

A shiver skidded over her skin. She didn't need to be around any man with the capacity to be dangerous. Still, she wondered what it would take to make him smile. Reaching out to draw her finger along his outline again, she stopped when her fingers met his lips.

Maybe Mr. November could remind her how good being with a real man could be, not some jerk who got off on hurting women. They would be working alone for several days, moving around the city. Almost nothing was as intimate to Lacey as staring down the barrel of her lens at someone, closing in, finding the shot.

It was New York City. Anything could happen.

SLOPE OF HIS CROUP, HUH? Would she be asking to check his teeth or feeling him up for spavins and thorough-pins and other physical faults before they were done? Jarod Wyatt shook his head, mostly amused. The idea of her feeling him up wasn't an entirely unappealing one, and at least she knew something about horses. He hadn't expected that from a city girl.

He stood in the dark corner of the *Bliss* studio, fascinated by the conversations he'd overheard, and more so with the woman who couldn't seem to keep her hands off him—or off his picture, anyway.

The smaller, dark-haired girl with the lusty sense of humor walked out the back, leaving the blonde—the photographer—standing alone in perfect silhouette against the white wall. She was lanky and somewhat coltish in build, but she moved gracefully. Her fingers were long and thin like the rest of her, though beneath the khakis and black T-shirt, he could see she had her share of curves.

Jarod had only been to New York once before, on the day after the bombings. The empty spot on the skyline still kicked him in the chest because he'd stood in the middle of it for several days and those were memories he wasn't likely to ever forget. He wasn't sure what he expected to feel coming back. Mostly it was good to see the city had recovered, that it was busy and teeming with life, the way it should be.

On the approach, he hadn't been able to take his eyes off the spot where the Towers used to be, but he noted driving in that there was so much life here, nothing could ever completely erase it. New York was a place unique unto itself, and if he wasn't here for such a ridiculous reason, he might enjoy the visit. He loved the scrub desert and wide-open spaces of Texas. His home was a part of his soul. Still, he enjoyed getting away every now and then, just like anyone else. Cities had their advantages.

He'd also been told there was a decent place that did

Texas barbecue better than he could find in his home state. He didn't want to believe it, but he had the address in his PDA and hoped to find out for himself.

Feeling a little like a Peeping Tom, he figured he should make himself known. He'd stayed to the back when he'd walked in, not wanting to interrupt, but now there wasn't any reason to lurk, except that he was enjoying the view.

Clearing his throat gently to signal his presence, he stepped forward from the hallway where he'd been standing. She whipped around, obviously startled, and he froze. Her posture signaled fright to him. Not a jump or a gasp of broken concentration, but her big eyes landed on him with a look that he'd seen far too often. Fear. Momentary panic.

He put his hands up, calming, showing he was no threat.

"Sorry, didn't mean to scare you, ma'am. I'm Lt. Jarod Wyatt, Texas Rangers, El Paso division— November, as you have me up on your board there," he said with a healthy dose of Texas charm and sincere chagrin. The picture reminded him why he was here, and it made his eyes roll every time he thought about it.

"You're not due until tomorrow," she said starkly, sounding a bit choked, as if trying to breathe correctly. Was she always this jumpy? She'd mentioned Nevada. Maybe she wasn't a city girl as he'd assumed.

"I took an early flight. Thought I'd stop by and check the place out. The door was open, and a secretary pushed me in this direction," he explained with just a hint of apology, then held out his hand. "Nice to meet you. I guess you're the photographer?"

Her eyes narrowed. "Why would you assume that?"

Whoops. He didn't want to let her know he'd been skulking in the corner for the past fifteen minutes. From the glare in her eyes, he wasn't sure that would go over too well.

Lacey Graham was a prickly number. *Pretty as could be, though,* he thought, taking in fine, almost porcelain features. Her eyes snapped dark green, and her mouth formed a perfectly pink rosebud, bare of any lipstick. Just what he preferred.

"Well, ma'am, it doesn't take much to figure out. You're here, in the studio, checking out the pictures on this big board, and speaking matter-of-factly, I heard you and your assistant talking when I first came in. Didn't want to interrupt," he offered by way of explanation and was glad to see her shoulders relax, her frame softening as she nodded.

"Sorry. It's not a good idea to sneak up on someone like that, especially after hours. I'm Lacey Graham, but I guess you already knew that."

Her hand was small in his, but strong. She had a firm grip, which triggered a small dart of unexpected arousal that he firmly pushed to the back of his mind.

"So this is the calendar spread, huh?" he said, scrutinizing the wall, trying to ignore his own picture among the others. He recognized one or two of the other guys, men he respected, and it helped him to not feel quite so cheesy about doing this. Not that he'd had much choice in the matter.

"Yep. These are just the PR shots we're using to play with. It will all change when we have the actual photos we choose for the final, but this gives me some idea what I want to do with each model."

"All due respect, but I'm not a model, and I'm betting none of these other guys are either."

He saw the corners of her lips twitch. "With all due respect back, Lieutenant, you *are* a model for the next week. It'll be fun, don't worry."

He frowned. "A week? I thought we'd spend a day taking pictures and I'd be on my way?"

She shook her head. "It will take more than that. We're shooting around the city, so I had to arrange for permissions to use various locations for each model. Some we have to get to at crazy times of day, they have to clear them out for a few hours, and that needs planning. Then I'd like to do some unposed, candid shots. The letter we sent stated the time requirements clearly."

He took a breath, shoved his hands in his pockets. He wasn't going to admit he'd been in a bitch of a mood about having been ordered to do this in the first place, and when the letter had come in the mail he'd ditched it, thinking he'd get out of the whole deal. His superiors had made him realize differently. Even law enforcement cared about public image these days. Far too much, in his view.

"I guess I figured it wouldn't take that long," he said, wincing slightly at the idea of this taking up so much time. "It's just a few pictures."

She laughed then, and he was struck by the sound, how

lively and natural it was. He had a feeling she used it a lot.

"It's much more than that. We need to cover a lot of ground, and I want to cover all four seasons from all models, since I may change my mind as to who gets placed where in the final analysis. This is a big deal, Lieutenant. I want this calendar to be a wild success."

"Good for your career, huh?"

Her posture stiffened again, and she tipped up her chin, nodding shortly. "Absolutely. Probably won't hurt yours any, either."

He didn't answer that. This had nothing to do with his career, but he wasn't going to get into a pissing match with the pretty lady.

"We'll be doing a group shot at the end at Ground Zero. You'll have to come back up for that, probably. Any problems there?"

"I guess not. Should there be?"

"Some of the guys weren't sure they could go back, to the site, I mean."

"I'm fine. Unless I happen to be out in the scrub chasing down felons, getting back here for a day shouldn't be difficult. As long as it's only a day," he warned. His supervisors had told him to do whatever the magazine needed, and this didn't come off his vacation time, so he found it hard to argue.

She peered up at him through thick lashes. "You hungry, Lieutenant?"

"Call me Jarod. And, yeah, I could go for something."

"If you want, I know some good places. Let me

close up here, and we can have our initial consult over some pizza or whatever you prefer. My treat."

His blood warmed more than it should, but there was no way he was turning down her invitation. He was curious about this beautiful photographer. No doubt she was smart. She was cagey, too, and she also had no qualms about meeting him eye to eye. She had a well-used laugh. All in all, an intriguing package.

"Sure, sounds good. I have to check in at my hotel, though."

"Where'd you book?"

"The Affinia. Not far from here."

"You'll like it. I'll meet you in the lobby in an hour, then?"

He reached up, tipped his hat. Her eyes followed his gesture so closely, as if she was already mentally taking him apart frame by frame. It was disconcerting.

"See you in an hour."

2

LACEY COULDN'T QUITE stifle the riff of excitement that hastened her movements as she rushed back to her loft and jumped in the shower to get ready to meet Lieutenant Wyatt in thirty minutes.

She'd nearly had a coronary when he'd walked up behind her in the studio. The man moved like a big cat. She hadn't heard a step on the hard acrylic floors, but how long had he been there? How much had he heard of Jackie's conversation with her? She shrugged. She'd said nothing that she felt ashamed of…well, there was the *thrusting* thing…but Jackie had come up with that one.

Lt. Jarod Wyatt was astounding in real life. The picture had muted the overall effect of absolutely radiant masculinity. She'd completely forgotten everything else—who she was, where she was—when he'd reached up, tipped the brim of his hat and smiled at her….

Oh, my.

She wasn't prone to fluttering around men, but Jarod Wyatt was fully deserving of it. He was stunning in person.

He also touched something deeper, a chord of comfort and familiarity. It seemed odd, having just met him, but he reminded her of the men she'd grown up with in Nevada. Big, capable men who put a premium on being gentlemanly, and who could be gentle. Like her dad, her uncles and cousins. Lacey had known plenty of good men, and only one bad, so she counted herself fortunate.

There was a sense of polish about Jarod Wyatt, too, though. He'd gone to college, for one thing. She knew from his profile that he had a master's in criminology, and he had some background in forensics. It was probably why they'd pulled him in on 9/11, beyond the sheer need for manpower. He wasn't just any cowboy cop.

It was why she'd asked him to dinner. That, and because she wanted to look at him more, to study him the way an artist would study any subject. He would be pure joy to photograph. Her mind was already placing him in poses, in settings.

A few of which were X-rated and included her bedroom.

She smiled, reaching for a towel and wiping down briskly. God, it was *good* to feel this way, if only for a moment. To look forward to a man's company again, even though it was only business over pizza. Maybe this was a good sign.

Grabbing black, formfitting pants, she tugged on a pair of heels and a hot-pink T-shirt with a colorful, fringed vest, assessing herself in the mirror.

If she were honest, she knew it was an outfit meant to draw a man's eye. A particular man's eye in this case. She nibbled her lip, suddenly apprehensive. So he was a good-looking guy—she should still be careful. Was it smart to have agreed to meet him, a stranger, for dinner? What did she really know about him, after all?

She shook off the doubts and their chilling effect. It was just business, some pizza and conversation. She'd wear this same outfit if anyone had suggested meeting her for dinner that evening. A lot of her clothes were colorful and funky and often drew attention. She wasn't going to second-guess it. This was who she was.

The phone rang, and she contemplated not bothering with it. She had to meet Jarod, and contrary to popular wisdom about keeping men waiting, Lacey was never late. She was obsessively punctual, in fact.

Making sure she had her wallet, she dug around to transfer her stuff to a smaller purse as she answered the phone.

"Hello?"

"Lacey?"

"Yes?"

"This is Gena, from Legal Aid in L.A.?"

She froze in place. Legal Aid had handled her case back in Los Angeles, since she couldn't afford a high-priced lawyer. Her family would have paid, but she didn't want them to know what happened. She told them she'd changed her name for business reasons, to maintain privacy from her work. She hated lying to them, but it was better than having them worry about her.

"Hi, Gena, what's up?" She tried to sound casual, cheerful, but it felt as if her stomach was in her throat.

"Listen, there's no need to worry, I want to emphasize that first. You should know that Scott Myers was released from his sentence to finish his probation on house arrest. He's out of prison, but he's still in California, and he won't be able to leave a predetermined schedule of home and work for fourteen more months."

"No," was all Lacey could breathe before Gena continued.

"Please, don't worry. He's wearing a personal monitoring device. He won't be able to find you, and probably won't bother, given his profile, the steps you've taken and your history. Still, if he attempts to contact you in any way, your restraining order is still in force, even under your new name, so let us know, okay? I don't want to upset you, but we like to make sure you know what's going on."

Lacey's breathing seemed cut off and she swallowed, her previous cheer evaporating as she found the air to mumble an answer before she hung up.

Scott was free.

He shouldn't have been released for another eighteen months, she recalled. The night he left Lacey unconscious on her kitchen floor he'd gone to a local bar and started a fight there, causing several thousand dollars of damage and other injuries. Luckily, the combined charges had sent him away for a while.

Lacey breathed deeply, calming herself. She had to listen to Gena, who wouldn't bullshit her. Scott wouldn't come after her. Still, when he'd left her lying there, broken and bruised, he'd made it clear he thought she was dead. His only comment upon finding out she wasn't was relief that he wouldn't be charged with murder.

She was far away now, new city, new name. The calendar project didn't really put her in the public eye—she was behind the scenes. *Bliss* wouldn't give out her personal details. She was safe, she reassured herself, standing frozen with the phone in her hand for several minutes.

Eyeing the door, the dark city streets that she usually loved so much suddenly seemed ominous. Anxiety gripped her at the thought of going out. With a stranger, no less.

What had she been thinking? Hadn't she learned anything from her previous mistakes?

She had no idea who Jarod Wyatt was, and just because he had an impressive official record, that didn't mean squat. Plenty of cops, firemen, doctors—all kinds of men—were closet crazies. More dangerous because of their outward appearance, because they had power and liked to use it. That's how it had been with Scott. Witty, handsome, successful…with all of that violence hiding under the surface.

She put her purse down, started to take her vest off, but stopped, pausing in the center of her living room.

This was important, her heart told her. She had a big choice to make.

Was she going to hide in her apartment and her studio for the rest of her life?

No. She didn't want to be that person.

The fear was just an emotional response, a *good* response, so the counselor at the hospital had reassured her. It would keep her alert and keep her safe, but she couldn't let it run her life. Good fear, bad fear. She had to remember the difference.

Jarod Wyatt was a man she'd be working with

closely, and she couldn't let her personal demons get in the way of her success on this job. His record was impeccable, and she'd been alone with him earlier and hadn't felt the least bit afraid. She'd been excited about seeing him tonight—maybe a little too excited—so now she knew to throttle that back so she didn't give the wrong impression. But she would still go.

She'd meet him in a populated, well-lit place for some pizza, talk work and welcome him to the city. Enjoy having his company for a few hours. She'd be friendly, professional and keep clear boundaries. Then she'd come home and put this all out of her mind.

She needed to keep things in perspective—it wasn't as if Jarod had asked her out, and he hadn't indicated anything other than casual friendliness. He was just a guy, another model.

No big deal.

JAROD STEPPED OUT of the elevator of the very nicely appointed hotel and smiled at a group of older women who watched him walk by. He smiled at them and touched his fingers to the brim of his hat. The group seemed to get a kick out of it.

He saw the beacon of Lacey's fuchsia shirt immediately as she stood poised by the entrance, looking around furtively. A glance at his watch told him he was five minutes early, and she'd obviously changed her clothes, so she couldn't have been waiting long. After his surprise appearance earlier, he approached carefully, making sure she had ample time to see him. She turned, smiling falsely, overbrightly.

Did she regret making plans with him?

He was perfectly happy to explore the city on his own, but he also looked forward to some company, someone to share the sights with for an evening. She'd seemed interested and friendly at the studio. He wondered what had changed.

"Hi there," he said casually, looking out at the streets bustling with early-evening traffic. The noises were muted here in the lobby. Though he could spend long days and nights in the desert enjoying nothing but the silence of the sand and the stars, he found the energy of the city stimulating, as well.

Or maybe it was the woman standing just a foot away, in spite of the tension stiffening her very nicely built form. Something about her had his blood circulating with a low, warm hum through his system, but he wasn't sure she was having the same reaction.

"You okay?" he found himself asking.

"Sure. Why do you ask?"

"You seem…strung a little tight."

She frowned, and shrugged. "Just distracted. Busy day, a lot on my mind."

The message underneath the cool reply really said "mind your own business" and wasn't lost on him. If this was going to be the mode of conversation, he was in for a long evening.

"How about a drink first? I could use something to warm up. Chilly out there tonight."

"I think it's going to be an early winter this year."

"You said you wanted to shoot seasonal photos— how is that possible when it's already October?" he

asked as they walked to the bar. She hadn't said yes or
no to the idea of a drink, but he wasn't lying about
wanting one. She didn't object as they headed in that
direction.

"Mostly we'll use props, how you're dressed, that
kind of thing. Then the postproduction guys can work
their magic, too. The photo will be mostly you and not
so much background. So for a July shot you might
wear trunks, and we'll work it that it looks summery."

"Even if I'm freezing my ass off in reality?"

"Yeah." She smiled then, and laughed. "Welcome to
the cruel world of modeling."

He ordered a whiskey, neat, and asked her if she
wanted anything, surprised when she ordered the same.
His eyebrows lifted as they tilted their glasses toward
each other and she swallowed hers in one throw, closing
her eyes as if she'd needed it more than he did. He
hadn't realized how pale she was until the warmth from
the whiskey infused her skin with a pink glow.

Something had happened between the time he'd left
and now, but he didn't feel free to inquire. He was a
stranger, a visitor that she was nice enough to spend
some time with because they had to work together. That
was it.

Maybe not, maybe more, whispered the hum in his
body. He ignored it. He wasn't opposed to having some
fun with a willing woman while he was here, but he
wasn't about to complicate matters with the prickly
photog—unless she offered an invitation—but she
wasn't being too inviting at the moment.

So why was he enjoying the view of the very feminine swell beneath the stylish top, taking advantage while her eyes were closed?

"You want to get some pizza? I know a place that has the best in the city," she said, opening her eyes just as he looked back up. *Almost caught staring,* he thought, feeling about seventeen.

Her green eyes were luminous, maybe in part from the whiskey, but she was a natural beauty, indeed. He waited before answering, questioning whether this was a good idea, but he'd already agreed. Jarod wasn't in the habit of backing out on a woman when he promised to spend an evening with her.

"Pizza? That sounds good. Must be a hundred pizza places here, but you know the best one, huh?"

He winced internally. Small talk was not his strength.

She grinned, seeming more relaxed. "Yes, I do, as a matter of fact. It's an amazing experience that will shift your entire perspective on what the dish means. The place is a hole-in-the-wall that tourists never find, so you're in for a treat. We'll pick up a bottle of vino on the way because they don't serve drinks. You have to bring your own."

"I like a lady with a plan," he agreed, glad she seemed to be loosening up.

"If you want to go up the Empire State Building at night, we could do that, too, after dinner—we'll be shooting up there. You afraid of heights?"

He shook his head as they walked out into the cool evening. "No. Heights aren't a problem. But you don't have to take me sightseeing. I figured this was a business dinner."

Her cheeks became warmer, and he realized his statement didn't quite come out the way he meant it.

"I meant—"

"No, no, you're right—this is a business dinner," she said easily, but didn't meet his eyes.

How could things be so weird and awkward, hot and cold, with a woman he'd just met two hours ago? Jarod was usually good with women. He enjoyed them as friends and lovers, and never had such tension or foot-in-mouth disease before. This one had him tripping over himself, and it wasn't a great experience.

They popped into a liquor store where Lacey seemed to be on a first-name basis with the owner and he handed her a Chianti that he knew she liked. Jarod insisted on paying.

"Fine, but the pie is on me," she said, and while it wasn't his habit to let women pay for a date, he agreed. It was her city, her pizza place, her expense account, he figured.

They walked a few blocks and turned in through a glass door painted white in order to be opaque into a deep, narrow room that was brightly lit, but nothing fancy. Small, round plastic tables hugged a stark white wall that featured signed pictures of various New Yorkers, many famous, others he didn't know.

"Interesting spot. I would never have guessed from the street this was even here."

"Best-kept secret."

She must be right as they had to navigate the narrow space between the counter and the tables to the far end to find an open table. The place was packed, and the rich aromas and sizzling pies he spotted on people's tables had his mouth watering.

Locating an empty table, they sat in plastic chairs that he hoped were sturdy as he settled his large frame into one. The napkins were paper, from a metal dispenser next to a small vase with some fake flowers. He wasn't a fancy guy, but he had to assume all of the money and talent in the place went into the food, not the decor.

"So this is your favorite place, huh?"

"Isn't it great?" She was all smiles again. If he were prone to it, her mercurial changes would make him seasick, she seemed to shift back and forth so often.

"I found it completely by accident. I was just passing by one night and someone opened the door. The smell of the sauce and spices had me making a U-turn to come in and see where it was coming from. It's bare bones, but cozy. Warm. And the owners are really nice people."

"Probably a gold mine, as well. Can't be much overhead," he commented.

"I bet you're right. Locals call it the Pizza Room, though I don't think it actually has an official name. If you get takeout, it's just a plain brown box, no logo. They don't do delivery and aren't in the directory."

He grinned, liking the simplicity of it. Lack of marketing was probably the best marketing of all in a world drowning in logos.

"I'm glad you decided to show me one of the city's secrets," he said, meaning it. This was much more his speed than some froufrou bistro or someplace where food arrived under silver domes.

"How hungry are you? One pie or two?"

"Are you going to eat?"

She stared at him, dumbfounded. "What? Of course I'm going to eat. Why do you think I'm here?"

"I meant, you're so thin, and given your profession, I thought you might be an 'eat salad and smell the real food' type."

She looked as if she couldn't believe his brashness, and then burst out laughing. At least he hadn't upset her.

"Ranger, I can put it away. Don't underestimate me there. I am blessed with what my father used to call a hummingbird's metabolism—small animal, eats a lot. No animal has a faster metabolism. I can probably eat damned near my own weight in this pizza."

"Is that right?"

She nodded and gave the waitress their order—two pies—after grabbing a few plastic cups from the counter for their wine and a conversation about the owner's new grandchildren.

"You seem to know everyone—I always thought New Yorkers were cold and distant."

"C'mon, you've been here before, so you know different. But anyway, I'm not a native. It's a big city, and it has its share of attitude, but I've found the people here to be some of the friendliest I've ever met. It's huge and intimidating, but you find your own corner and settle in. I've known small towns a lot less friendly."

He had to admit that was true. "Where do you come from originally?"

"Nevada. My parents owned a ranch there."

"Seriously?" He sounded surprised, even though

he'd heard her reveal that fact earlier. She seemed tickled by his feigned reaction.

"Yep. Grew up with the desert, rattlesnakes, horses and cattle—probably not unlike you, huh?"

"I actually didn't grow up on a ranch. Just a small house outside Corpus Christi. I didn't learn to ride until I took a summer job on a local cattle ranch and got hooked."

"I thought everyone in Texas was born in a saddle," she said, obviously teasing.

"My father was a good horseman, but he was all cop."

"Law enforcement runs in the family?"

"Yep. My sister is a Federal Marshall, Dad's a lifelong Ranger, though he'll be set to retire next year. He's not taking that well."

"Your file said you were in the El Paso Division?"

"Yeah. I was transferred a few years ago. Dad is still over in Corpus Christi. My sister is based in Dallas, but she's constantly traveling."

"That's a lot. How does your mother handle it?"

"She didn't. She took off when I was about thirteen after putting up with it for as long as she could. I can't blame her, not entirely."

"Really?"

"The job is tough, comes with a lot of risks, makes having a family hard, just like any cop's life does. My mother couldn't take the stress. It happens."

"I suppose. I'm sorry to hear it, though. Are you still in touch?"

"You writing an exposé or taking pictures?" he

snapped back, and noticed too late that he shouldn't have. She'd just hit a nerve.

He'd always felt responsible for his parents' breakup, though as an adult he knew it wasn't true. Still, it was hard for him as a boy to ignore that his mother had taken off shortly after he'd said he wanted to be a Ranger, just like his father. Hard to convince a kid it wasn't his fault, even though his dad had tried.

"It helps me take better pictures if I get to know you," she said evenly, but her eyes didn't meet his.

"Apologies, Lacey. Sore spot. Shouldn't take it out on you," he said, and she looked up again, her eyes forgiving him. "But, no, we lost contact with her a few years after she left. She stayed in touch for a while, but I guess her new life took her elsewhere."

"I'm sorry about that. And I didn't mean to pry."

"I know."

Thankfully their pizzas arrived, taking up all of the space on the table and capturing their attention for a good while.

"Wow, this is amazing," he said, his senses in heaven between the pizza and the wine. "I mean, my God…what do they do? I could eat only this for the rest of my days," he crooned, meaning it.

"Told ya." She smiled, as she kept her promise and put away her share of pizza. He couldn't figure out where she fit it all.

"So, you want to talk about work?" he reminded her as they poured more wine. She wasn't tipsy by any means, but she was more relaxed and he liked it. The glow she had was real now, and the buzz of attraction in his head became a little louder. She was fun, and good company when she wasn't acting like something was about to bite her. Whatever cloud had been hanging over her earlier seemed to have lifted.

"That's what we've been doing. I like to get to know subjects before I shoot them, so I can put you into places, settings, poses that are going to really show the real you, not arrange you in some contrived position."

"I see. That's interesting." He was unsure of what else to say, slightly uncomfortable at being analyzed in this manner. He'd thought they were just having a good time. He sighed. "I'm not quite sure how all this model, photographer stuff works. It's a first, and hopefully a last, for me."

She grinned. "Maybe you'll get hooked. You could get catalog ads, newspaper, maybe even hit the catwalks," she teased. She was playful, something he liked in a woman, and in a bed partner. How playful would his pretty photographer be in the sack? He watched her lick some sauce from her fingers and thought about those long, thin fingers wrapping around him.

He had to stop or he wouldn't be able to stand up safely, and grabbed his drink and took a long swallow.

"I said it's time to go, dammit. I gotta get to work," a rough voice growled, interrupting them. The jovial conversation in the place dulled to a murmur. Everyone looked toward a tall twentysomething guy who stood and grabbed the woman with him by the wrist, pulling her up. She tugged her arm loose, telling him she wanted to stay and pack the rest of the pizza for takeout.

There were several beer bottles on his side of the table and his words were slurred as he objected again. It was obvious he'd had too much to drink.

When the guy lifted his hand toward her, Lacey went very still. Jarod, on the other hand, moved so quickly the guy didn't seem to realize he was there until he'd grabbed the man's arms and pinned them behind his back before he managed to deliver the blow.

"This is a nice place, and we're all enjoying a nice meal. You, however, are not behaving nicely," Jarod said in a voice that was dead calm.

"Let me go, you moth—"

"Uh-uh." Jarod yanked harder on the guy's arms, choking off the curse. "There are kids in here. Watch your words."

"Let him *go*," the girlfriend demanded, her hands on her hips as she stared at Jarod as if he were the enemy.

"Ma'am, are you okay?"

While the guy had gone still, the woman didn't seem to be intimidated by Jarod at all, and walked up as close as she could get to him.

"Why don't you mind your own damned business? Let him go so we can get out of here."

"He looked like he was about to slap you. You sure about me letting him go?" Jarod asked.

She glared at him as if he were nuts. "Don't I look sure? He don't mean no harm. He just gets worked up." She blew off Jarod's concern with a dirty look that brooked no argument.

Others sat down and Jarod let the guy's arms go, putting his hands up, backing off. When the thug turned on him with fiery eyes and appeared as if he might try throwing a punch, Jarod didn't move a muscle, but just stared. Something in his posture made the kid think twice. He and his girlfriend charged out the door, cursing. They left their pizza behind.

Jarod returned to the table, shaking his head.

"Unbelievable. I kept him from possibly hitting her and she defends him."

He sat down, eyes landing on Lacey. It was clear that something had changed. She was white as a sheet. Her irises were open and dark—a classic fight-or-flight response.

"Hey, you okay?"

She nodded, but when she put her fork down, her hand was shaking. Jarod reached across the table, put his hand over hers. It was ice-cold, he noticed, before she snatched it back.

"Want to talk about it? I can be a good listener."

That woke her up, and she blinked, as if coming alive. "No, I don't. I should get home," she stated flatly, and he felt properly put in his place. Thing was, he'd been put in his place plenty of times, and he pretty much knew when he didn't want to stay there.

"I'll walk you to your apartment," he offered, throwing down a few dollars to cover the bill.

"No!" she objected too strongly, and when she glanced at him he could swear she was afraid of *him*. Where had that come from?

"I just want to make sure you're safe, is all."

"I'll be fine. I'm just tired and have a bad headache, from the wine," she explained, standing and walking rapidly toward the door. When they got outside, she took several deep breaths and seemed to steady. He wasn't quite sure what to do or say.

"I'm sorry," she said, sounding more normal, though she examined the narrow street, up and down, as if she were expecting someone. "I guess I was a bit thrown by that episode. I'm not great with confrontation. It was good of you to step in, though."

"It's my job."

"Not here."

"Doesn't matter where I am. It's still my job."

She focused on his face, and studied him for a few long moments with those perfect green eyes.

He knew he wanted her. He didn't know how he'd manage it, but he was going to make it happen.

"You sure you don't want me to walk you back?"

She paused, but then nodded.

"I'm sure. I'll be fine."

It hit him then that she didn't want him knowing where she lived. She was afraid of him—or afraid of men, in general.

There were only a few good reasons women had for this kind of reaction, and thinking about any of them made Jarod's blood boil. The lady had some serious fear, and he knew he had to find out why. Then he'd make sure she had no reason to fear anything, least of all him.

"Fair enough, then," he said, knowing when to give in and when not to. "I guess I'll see you tomorrow for that appointment, and you can let me know more of what's expected of me?"

"Yes. Thanks," she said, though he wasn't exactly sure what she was thanking him for. He just nodded.

She walked off without another word, and he veered off in the direction of his hotel—at first.

Within a minute he looped back, caught sight of that hot-pink shirt and didn't take his eyes away from her the rest of the way. He kept his distance and watched. She checked her surroundings constantly, as if the devil himself were after her.

Jarod stayed with her until he saw her turn into a building. He waited, saw a light come on, didn't see her come out. Walking up closer, he noted the address, the spot, and committed it to memory. Only then did he walk back through the dark street to his own place, quietly planning to find out what had Lacey Graham so spooked.

3

JAROD SAT IN THE SUNLIGHT of the large hotel window, the city sprawled out below him while he perused the Net, making good use of the wireless connection that came with the room. He enjoyed touching base with law enforcement colleagues on various boards and Web sites, and he was taking an online course in further forensics study.

He didn't particularly want to become a forensics expert. He was more interested in chasing down perps directly, rather than investigating the mess they left behind; still, he found the material interesting.

Mostly.

Today, no matter how intently his eyes traveled over the words on the screen, his mind kept returning to the image of Lacey's green eyes. He loved her eyes, and the way she pushed her hands through her short blond hair every five minutes. She had hair like corn silk, soft-looking in spite of the blunt edges of the style she wore. He flexed his fingers unconsciously, thinking about touching it. The ring of his cell phone jostled him out of his fantasy, and he recognized the number as his captain's.

"Hey, Cap."

"Jarod. How are things in the big city?"

"Noisy. Busy. Damned good pizza, though."

Tom chuckled. Jarod liked him. He was a good man, no-nonsense, and had as much tolerance for political bullshit as Jarod did.

"Thought you might be out somewhere with twenty half-naked women draped over you for this calendar thing," Tom said lightly, razzing him. There would be no end to that when he got home.

"Nope, no women, just eleven other guys, unfortunately, except for the photographer, and she's pretty tough."

"Would have to be to deal with the likes of you." Tom laughed again. "Anyway, I'm calling about Darren Hill."

"What about him?"

"He jumped bail last night, thought you'd want to know."

Jarod cursed. Darren Hill was the worst of the worst, selling everything he could get his hands on to pay for drugs, including his six-year-old daughter. Jarod had intervened, and the girl had escaped serious harm in the nick of time, taken away and placed in a foster home. No one knew if she'd been born on American soil or not, but Hill claimed she was. Meanwhile, the mother was long gone. *Poor kid.* Jarod still felt a twist when he thought about it. Still, she had a real chance now, placed with a good family in Houston. Hopefully they would keep her permanently.

Jarod had a feeling they needed to be looking for the mother's body, unfortunately. Hill was scum.

"How the hell did he even make bail?"

"It was set high, but his drug-dealing friends must have come up with the cash."

"Great. That's just great." Jarod narrowed his eyes, peering out through the window. "Any idea which way he headed?"

"Pretty sure he wouldn't go back over the border—he wouldn't take that chance. And he has a bone to pick with you taking away the kid. We wouldn't want to ignore that."

"Oh, yeah, he was a really devoted father."

"It's about the power and control. You know that. You damaged his rep. He might be looking for revenge."

"Yeah, well, he can bring it on. I'll get the first flight back."

"No, you're out there until this calendar thing is finished—brass made no bones about that."

"Dammit, Tom, if Hill's looking for me, the easiest way for me to bring him in is to be there, not here."

"It's being handled, Jarod. Stay there, and enjoy being out of the line of fire for a bit."

"Tom—"

"Jarod, you know I don't care about this PR crap any more than you do, but the brass does care and you're supposed to be doing this. So do it."

"Aren't you the brass?"

"You know what I mean. We'll find Darren. The place does tend to run without you, you know," Tom added jokingly, and Jarod blew out a breath.

"Fine. Keep me up-to-date on what's happening?"

"You bet. By the way, you put any more thought toward taking that captain's position that's opening up? You're the perfect candidate. You'd have no problem getting through the interviews. I'd be happy to write you a rec."

Something nasty squeezed at Jarod's temples, and he told Tom the truth. "All due respect, and believe me, being asked to fill your shoes is an honor, but I don't know if I want that, Tom. I like where I am now. Too much paperwork comes with being a captain."

"Ain't that the truth," Tom agreed, laughing good-naturedly. "Still, there are more guys who can do your job, and not many as well suited as you are to this chair. You're a natural leader, Jarod. And captains are still hands-on much of the time. Better pay, too. Maybe a chance of living a little longer," Tom joked, having been in the captain's seat for ten years before recently being promoted to assistant chief.

Jarod knew Tom wanted him to take the spot, and it was getting harder to resist. "I'll think some more on it."

"Think faster. This has to be decided sooner than later."

"Will do."

They hung up, and Jarod rubbed his eyes, feeling tired. A restless night's sleep had done him no favors. He was going to have to make some decisions. His father wouldn't be happy if he turned down the promotion, yet it just didn't feel right. He should be excited, but for whatever reason, he wasn't. He liked what he did, and had never really thought about climbing the political ladder. He just wasn't ambitious that way.

Shaking his head, he set the thoughts aside and sat back down at his computer, distracting himself by typing Lacey's name into the search engine.

His conscience pricked at him a bit, but what of it? He was going to be working with the woman, and he was curious.

Surprisingly, he didn't find much. Wouldn't a person in her line of work have more Internet presence? Promotions, articles, displays of their work, a Web page? She did have a Web page connected to *Bliss,* but it was basic info, a few samples of her previous work—impressive—but most notably, no pictures of herself. Wasn't that odd, for a photographer?

He shrugged. Maybe he was off base. However, following an instinct, he accessed a database used by law enforcement to do background checks and paused before typing in her name. He had no call to do this, no professional reason.

No, his reasons were personal. The lady had been seriously stressed about something. Jarod didn't think for a minute that she was a criminal, but she was hiding something; he could smell it. And he wanted to know why she was so afraid, and of what.

He wouldn't dig too deep, only see if anything curious came up. Then he'd leave it at that. There was a fine line between curiosity and concern, and invasion of privacy.

He didn't know if he was relieved or not to find that on the surface query nothing came up. Not even a speeding ticket or a court date. However, Lacey Brown had changed her name to her mother's maiden name,

Graham, upon arriving in New York City. She'd renewed all of her official IDs, license, Social Security, etcetera, all at once.

When she'd come here, she'd reinvented herself— it piqued Jarod's attention as to why. It could be as simple as her not liking her last name for starting a new career, or perhaps she'd been married, and returned to her mother's name when she'd left the relationship.

Lacey Brown. He couldn't see where that was such an objectionable name—why wouldn't she want her father's name? She'd sounded happy with her child-hood from what Jarod could tell when he'd heard her talking about growing up on the ranch in Nevada, and so why the switch?

Some people did business by adopting a business name, a DBA, "doing business as" but Lacey had changed her entire identity, officially. When someone took such a drastic step, there was usually a big reason why.

The need to know was balanced by the need to stick to professional ethics. He'd already crossed the line slightly, and he wouldn't pry any further, regardless of the temptation. Closing the database and the computer before he gave in to his baser impulses, he sat quietly, wonder-ing.

Other than criminal activity, the other obvious option was that she was hiding or running away from something or someone who scared her. It brought him to simmering anger to think about that, and he almost opened the database again, wanting to know. If Lacey was afraid of something, he could help. What would he find if he checked into Lacey Brown's past?

If she wanted him to know, she'd tell him, he reminded himself sternly. He had no compelling reason to pry into her business. None at all.

Standing up, he headed for the shower, needing to get out of the room. He was meeting with Lacey in two hours, and he was looking forward to it a little more than he should be.

IN GOOD TIME Lacey finished two of her interview consultations, one with a member of their own FDNY and another with a member of the California Highway Patrol. Things were moving ahead and a spirit of excitement was only dimmed by the black cloud of knowing Scott was out of jail. She'd barely slept all night, paranoid and stressed, and feeling like an idiot for how she'd acted with the Ranger in the pizza place.

She glanced at Jackie, who was across the studio, but it was hopeless. Jackie was far too busy flirting with one of New York's best to notice Lacey. Lacey frowned—Jackie was a free spirit and probably just used to playing the game at work, but it was hard to believe she was in much of a relationship if she was acting like that....

And look at me, little Miss Critical, who hasn't been near a man in months, Lacey chastised herself.

To say she was feeling out of sorts was an understatement, her day full of surprises so far. The execs from *Bliss* had wanted her to walk them through the current setup, and though she'd tried to explain that it could change once she had all the early photos in, they had seemed happy, if not thrilled, with the early work.

Her stomach turned; she needed them to be thrilled, ecstatic even, but Lacey was sure that the female exec in Marketing, Nina, would never like anything she did completely. There was an innate animosity there that Lacey didn't understand, but it happened sometimes. Personalities clashed for whatever reason.

Lacey was determined to do better than her best, and wow them no matter what.

It wasn't going to be a smooth morning by the looks of things. Jackie was busy and had messed up a few scheduling details. Assisting Lacey wasn't her only duty at the magazine, so Lacey tried to be understanding. Now there was a very annoyed California Highway Patrol officer demanding to know why his appointment had changed—again.

Lacey tried to placate him, but she just couldn't fit him in at the moment, and needed to push his shoot back until she was done with Jarod. The patrol officer wasn't happy about it. The guy was not Mr. Sunshine, and Lacey couldn't blame him for being irritated, but there was nothing else to be done.

Jarod was due here any second, and she needed time to prepare. She wanted to start by taking some studio shots of Jarod, to get a feel for him, so to speak. She'd thought about that in more ways than one the evening before, until the incident in the café had thrown her.

She couldn't help it, but seeing someone manhandled just brought back flashes of Scott. Seeing Jarod step in had been both exciting and frightening. She didn't know what to think of it.

Left to handle it all on her own for the time being,

Lacey turned back to the disgruntled highway patrol officer and offered a friendly smile, hoping it would dim his temper. It did, maybe too well. She realized while she'd been looking toward Jackie, the guy's eyes hadn't moved from her chest.

Great. Like she needed this.

"Listen, Officer Bridges, if you go talk to my assistant—"

"She looks busy," he said, not even glancing at Jackie. He stepped closer, turned on a little charm of his own. "I'd rather talk to you. Maybe we could have dinner, work this out, find some time to squeeze me in. I'm not opposed to a private session, you know?"

The suggestive way he said the words and leaned in made Lacey reflexively pull back, his intimidating closeness unwelcome. Her back was, however, literally against the wall, and he planted a big hand just a few inches to the right of her head.

Panic was reflexive.

She tried to keep her cool in spite of her racing heart, but wanted to draw the line at his suggestive tone and mannerisms. She was in a public place, and in no danger. "Back off, please."

He grinned. "Aw, c'mon, sweetheart. Surely you and I can work something out that's good for both of us? I came all the way across the country to be here…can't we make it worth my while?"

She weighed her options quickly, and decided she wouldn't stand much chance of pushing him away, his chest was massive. She started to duck under his arm, when a cool voice stopped her mid duck.

"The lady said back off. I suggest you listen."

She looked underneath the officer's massive arm to see a pair of well-fitted jeans…and cowboy boots.

Straightening, she met Jarod's eyes, and was shocked that the warm brown of his gaze could turn so cold.

"Why don't you get in line, Tex," the California officer said dismissively over his shoulder.

Lacey found herself suddenly standing alone, free from the arm that had been by her head. The next thing she knew, two large and extremely agitated men were facing off with each other just six feet in front of her nose, seething at each other like large, angry bulls. She moved quickly, keeping her distance, her heart pounding, and she made it to Jackie's side.

"Call security," she said, her voice tight. She noted with relief the fireman who'd been talking to Jackie heading toward the two men with calming gestures.

"That won't be necessary," Jarod said, overhearing her, and acknowledging the fireman. "Everything is under control, and Chippie here is just leaving."

The young Californian started to object, but took in the measure of the Texas Ranger and fireman standing before him and broke eye contact first. He cursed, pointing a finger in Lacey's direction.

"Fine, I'm outta here and not coming back to this hole of a city. You can find someone else for this stupid calendar," he said, spitting and sending red-faced looks toward all of them as he stormed out. "You had me too late in the lineup anyway. Don't know what the hell you're doing."

Jackie's voice broke through Lacey's haze, but her eyes remained glued to the men.

"Hey, what's up? You're shaking like a leaf."

Lacey blinked a few times, and realized everyone was staring at *her* now, not the men. Awareness kicked in.

"I'm fine," she said automatically.

"You don't seem fine. That guy really got to you, huh?"

"He was just being stupid," she said, her throat feeling dry.

"Well, Mr. November took care of him just fine, with a little help from Mr. April, who, by the way, is perfectly single and lives here in New York," Jackie said playfully. Lacey barely heard, her eyes still on Jarod as he spoke with the firefighter.

"They make quite a pair, huh?"

"Uh, yeah, sure."

"Mr. November sure seems interested in impressing you—he looked like he wanted to wallop that guy."

Which is exactly what bothered Lacey. She liked Jarod, as much as she knew about him, but he had an aggressive streak and wasn't the type of guy to hold back. This was New York, not the Wild West.

"You should ask him out," Jackie added.

"I can't date these guys, Jackie. It's not professional. At least until their shoot is done. The magazine must have some kind of policy about that."

"For regular staff, yes, but not regarding contract and freelance employees, which includes you and those two gorgeous hunks over there. So it's fair game."

"I need to get November into the studio for some inside shots," Lacey said, dropping the subject and focusing on work again.

"Hey, do you want to tell me what has you so freaked out, Lace?" Jackie inquired.

Frowning more deeply, Lacey studied her lens as she polished it. "I'm just tired and stressed. I need this to go perfectly. We're off to a bumpy start and we need to get this under control."

Jackie's expression soured, and Lacey regretted sounding so harsh.

"No problem. I'll get back on it."

Lacey closed her eyes.

"Jackie, wait. I'm sorry. I just hate getting rattled when I really need to concentrate. This calendar is my big break, and I want it to be perfect," she explained.

"I get it, and I'm sorry, too. I've been enjoying the fringe benefits too much. But Ken's been such a crank lately, it's a relief to come to work, you know?"

Lacey wasn't sure if Jackie wanted to say more about her troubles with her boyfriend, but now wasn't the time, and she wasn't exactly someone to hand out romantic advice anyway.

"I hope it works out," she offered and lifted her camera, studying the serious profiles, angular features, and sharp eyes of the two men. She snapped a few quick shots of them as they talked. Candid shots, when people weren't posing or looking, had always been her favorites to take. A moment captured in time that often showed the truth about the person being photographed.

"Well, you have no shortage of material to work

with, that's for sure. Just let me know what you need to make it happen." Jackie slipped back into her professional role, and Lacey felt her shoulders relax.

"I'm moving to studio one—could you tell Jarod to join me in about ten minutes? I'll be ready for him then."

"Sure. You got it," Jackie said, though Lacey could feel her assistant staring as she left the room.

She needed the few minutes of quiet before being around anyone again, to get her bearings, to distance herself from her churning stomach and riled nerves. The cop wouldn't have hurt her, he was just being obnoxious. Lacey had come across worse in her dating life, and had usually laughed it off. This time, she hadn't. Was it always going to be this way?

No. She wouldn't allow it. It was simply the aftereffect of the news about Scott. And it had to stop. Now.

Taking a deep breath, she cleared her mind and stepped backward, finding herself up against a solid wall of muscle.

"Whoa, careful there. You okay?"

Jarod's hands were on her shoulders, the rest of him warm and hard against her back as her nervous system sparked to life like a car battery with a new charge.

Warmth from his touch traveled over her skin. He leaned in, speaking by her ear, and she closed her eyes as his voice filled her senses.

"Lacey, are you okay? You seemed upset out there."

The reminder had her pulling away, rubbing her hands over her arms and meeting his gaze furtively.

"I'm fine. I just… I don't like… Nothing. I'm fine. Let's get to work."

She looked away from Jarod's curious gaze and set to messing with lights and her camera, placing a small wooden stool at the center of the room, in front of a few gray-and-white screens.

"Can you please sit there? Don't pose or do anything particular. Hang out and let me get a sense of shooting you."

Jarod agreeably made his way to the seat and turned to her with a smile.

"This okay?"

"Sure," she said, shrugging and taking a few preliminary shots.

She fell into her groove easily, everything else taking a backseat as she studied him through the lens, taking in his features as if she'd never seen him before. Zooming in, she noted the lush fringe of lashes and framed his eyes only, liking the laugh lines carved into tanned skin and the flecks of color in his cocoa irises that only her camera would pick up.

Click.

Moving down, she saw the beginnings of his beard and realized his nose had been broken.

"How'd you break your nose?" she asked, her fingers navigating the camera's controls quickly and naturally as she readjusted her shots. The space between them dissolved through the closeness of the focus, and she could have been touching him as much as touching the machine in her hands.

Click.

"Which time?" he asked with a sardonic slant to his lips.

"The last time."

"Kidnapping standoff. A guy held a woman and her daughter in their apartment with a shotgun for eighteen hours. When we went in, some of us went for him, drew the fire, while others got the victims out. Turned out the gun wasn't loaded. The guy was strung out, though, and it took six of us to get him out of there. I caught his knee to the face while restraining him."

Jarod's eyes became so serious as he spoke, the irises expanding and the brighter flecks of gold seeming to disappear momentarily, swallowed by his memories. She widened out the shot.

Click, Click, click.

Amazing.

Her blood sizzled the longer she listened, the closer she looked.

"Knee to the face, sounds fairly painful," she commented briefly to keep him going.

To that, he smiled more widely, and the camera responded with an explosion of action that took her to the end of the roll. She held her breath the entire time.

Finding she needed to catch her breath, she stood and reached for some more film.

"You can relax for a second," she said, not looking up, needing to get hold of an emotional response she didn't understand. She loved to shoot and always enjoyed the rush, but it had never affected her physically, never like this. With Jarod, the necessary distance between photographer and subject was made of gossamer, thin and fading.

"No digital?" he asked casually, standing, but not

joining her. She could feel him watching her and it was disconcerting. Normally, the positions were reversed, the subject of her shoots being the one studied and explored.

"I like film. *Bliss* has supplied me with a digital, and I'll do some sessions with that, too. Part of my agreement to do the calendar was based on being able to work in film. Digital is just not the same."

"How so?"

"With film you have to be aware of your limits, of how many shots you have, and then it takes physical maneuvering to make them work. They can still be manipulated on a computer, of course, but I like developing myself, and it's just more…"

"Personal," he supplied.

"Real." She spoke at the same time.

She glanced up and met his knowing look. She shuffled her step a little, trying to work away the warmth that gathered low in the pit of her abdomen, signaling how long it had been since she'd felt the things he was causing her to feel.

"Yes. Personal. Anyway, just do what comes naturally, and we'll be finished in a few minutes," she said somewhat breathlessly, to her dismay.

"Sure." He shoved his hands in his pockets and simply noted her with a steadiness that made her pull back the zoom, taking more comfortable, wide-angle shots.

God, he was gorgeous. The thought would not be denied, and the heat inside picked up intensity. She was in some kind of trouble.

"When do we start doing this for real?"

"Tomorrow."

"Here?"

"No, our first stop is Central Park."

"Do I get to keep my clothes on?" he asked cheekily, with a naughty sparkle in his eyes. She fumbled the camera, messing up the shot and frowning.

"Depends on whether you mean during or after the shoot," she said off the cuff, shocking herself. It was something the "old" her would have said without a second thought, and she couldn't repress a smile as she watched his rapid reaction.

Score one for Lacey. She still had it, apparently.

He didn't say anything else, and she finished the last roll of film, pleased with herself for the shots and for finding her own spark. Temptation quelled doubt for the moment.

Lieutenant Wyatt had something special, a mysterious quality that reached past her fears and sparked her former, playful spirit to life.

Did she dare?

This tall Texas cop might be good for her after all. He might be worth the chance, she thought, focusing hard on her camera, but she wasn't really paying attention to what she was doing; her hands moved automatically.

Maybe. Just maybe.

4

"THAT'S PERFECT, thanks," Lacey said, giving the thumbs-up on the props put in place by the small crew the magazine had sent out to get their first official calendar session under way.

It wasn't complex; she wanted natural photos that emphasized the masculine power of the models. The most handsome heroes in the country against the backdrop of the most powerful city in the world. She didn't want a lot of hokey items drawing attention away from Jarod. As if they could.

She noticed he hadn't arrived yet and peeked at her watch. He still had a few minutes, but he did like to cut it close, making her punctuality nerves bristle.

She wondered if he'd been as affected by their time in the studio the day before as she'd been, then chastised herself for the thought. How could he have been? She was the one with the camera, watching his every movement up close and personal through her lens. The details of his eyes, the shape of his mouth had followed into her dreams that night.

She'd almost called him, but had talked herself out of it. Instead, she stayed up late developing the pictures she'd taken, memorizing each one, telling herself they were no different than what she did for any other model, any other shoot. Details were her business, and Jarod happened to have particularly nice ones.

"We're all set," one of the prop guys told her after they'd set up some barricades fencing off the area to keep bystanders out of the shot and had raked colorful leaves into strategic positions. Thank God there wasn't any wind today.

A colorful blanket was positioned on the ground among the leaves, two wineglasses and a bottle poised perfectly, waiting for Jarod to complete the picture. A fall picnic in the park with a handsome Texas Ranger. It had been Jackie's idea, and pure genius. He'd sit alone, as if waiting for someone—and millions of women looking at the calendar would imagine they were the one he was waiting for. Exactly what Lacey intended. She wasn't sure if it was her own fantasy driving her direction, but as long as the shot worked, that's all that mattered. She wanted every woman in America thinking about joining Jarod on that blanket.

She played with the fantasy of sitting down there with him, herself, sheltered from view by the trees and the large boulder, the skyscrapers looming in the background sky… What would happen?

"A few of the prop guys are grabbing lunch. The stylist will prep Jarod as soon as he gets here, and we should be okay. Did he know the way? Should we have sent a car?" asked Jackie.

Lacey shrugged. "I offered. He said he'd get here on his own power—oh, wait—there. In the nick of time."

Both women turned to watch Jarod striding down the walk, emerging from one of the park's many tunnels into the dappled sunlight, looking like…well, Lacey wasn't sure she had the right words. Good thing she took pictures for a living.

"Wow," was all Jackie said, and turned back to tell the stylist their model had arrived.

You're a professional, cool it, Lacey lectured herself silently, her hormones begging to stand up and salute.

She'd asked Jarod to wear his official uniform today, and he'd informed her that unlike other police or fire departments, there really wasn't any official Ranger uniform. So, he'd come in the clothes he used as a dress uniform. Western-cut white shirt, dark tie, gray pants, belt and cowboy boots. A white hat. The clothes weren't that unusual, but the man who wore them made them seem more…elegant.

Powerful.

Lacey's fingers itched, and she lifted her camera, taking a few shots of him as he crossed the grass.

There wasn't a set of female eyes in the park that could turn away, and several guys looked on, too, for that matter. Some whistled. Several started gathering around the edges of the shoot as he arrived.

He seemed to have eyes only for her, though, and she had to admit that set her on fire, especially when he smiled. She might have smiled back, but couldn't risk it.

"Hi, there. Didn't know there'd be an audience," he said casually enough, hands on hips, peering at the gathering crowd through narrow eyes.

Lacey grinned a little wider. "It's New York. Something's always going on, and someone always wants to watch."

He laughed and shook his head. "Whatever you say. So how does this work?"

"We have the set put together, we'll use that first, with you in your dress uniform and then your casuals. Later, we can walk around the park and I'll get some candid shots. It will give me a variety to select from later."

"Casual?" He frowned. "I didn't bring any change of clothes."

"No problem—we have stuff we want you to wear, designer labels that paid to be in the calendar. Product placement, you know. You can see Jen, the stylist, for any last-minute touch-ups, and then we'll get started. You can change after."

"Stylist?"

"Yeah. Hair, makeup, clothes—she'll get you all set." Lacey felt a twinge of jealousy as she thought about the young, pretty stylist with her hands all over Jarod, and squelched it. Stupid.

"Makeup? I am not wearing makeup."

Blinking at him, she frowned. "Why not?"

He looked down at her, but didn't say a word.

Lacey stared in the face of his stalwart refusal to wear makeup, her aggravation rising—what was the big deal? But as she saw Jackie behind Jarod pointing to her watch, and then upward toward the sun, Lacey let it go. They were going to be dealing with shadows crawling across the scene if they waited much longer.

"Don't blame me if you look blotchy," she warned. "I'll deal with it."

Actually, she knew he wouldn't look blotchy at all, which was why she hadn't insisted more strenuously. The studio light had been more controlled, but she knew that the soft, indirect sunlight would be kind to Jarod's desert-tanned skin.

She watched Jackie instruct him about the shot, and cursed as her cell phone buzzed in her pocket. She'd forgotten to shut it off, as was her habit when she was shooting.

Unknown name and number. Again.

Her fingers turned cold as she ignored it, only to have the phone ring again a few seconds later, with the same result. Finally, she answered it. Nothing. Someone hanging on the line, not saying a word. Then, a soft male laugh, and a click. Her knees felt watery, and she turned her back to Jackie and Jarod. She took a minute, pretending to be on the phone, but really getting her bearings.

It was hard to tell from just a laugh, and the scratchy connection of what was probably a cheap, disposable cell phone didn't help. It could be anyone, but it was most likely Scott. It had to be.

It was only a phone call, she reassured herself. He was far away, under house arrest, and he couldn't do anything to her over the phone. If it continued, she'd call her lawyer and make it stop.

She didn't want to start anything, or give Scott any more reason to come back at her, so she'd wait and see. He was just baiting her. Letting her know he was out there. That was all. As if she'd ever forget.

She turned back around, blowing out a breath that teased her bangs, and shot a bright smile at Jarod, who was watching a little too closely with those hawklike eyes. She glanced around, gave a short nod.

"Okay, everyone, let's get to work."

JAROD HAD ONCE SPENT eighteen hours with his leg jammed in between rocks when he'd slipped while he'd been searching for a fugitive. His dad always said it was the little things that could kill you. Like slipping at the wrong moment while climbing rocks you'd been scaling since you were a kid.

He'd had enough water to keep himself going, but had dropped his radio about ten feet away and crushed his cell phone when he'd fallen. Basically, he'd been completely screwed; if not for keeping his gun, he might have been snake or wildcat bait, as well. Luckily, when he hadn't checked in, they came looking for him, saving him from death or having to do something unspeakable to free himself. He'd been hot, sunburned, dirty, sore, hungry and nearly dehydrated when they brought him back.

Still, that had been more fun than he was having right now, being primped and poked in public, bent this way and that, holding up a champagne glass to the camera and having to look…well, deserving of the wolf whistles and other comments that floated over from the crowd.

Lacey had actually used the phrase "come hither" until she realized it made him glare, not smile.

He'd have to get his gun and go shoot something when this was done, just to get his self-respect back.

"You're doing great," Lacey reassured him, changing out her film again and then switching over to her digital camera. How the hell many pictures did she need to take just to find one good one?

"Can you change clothes, and we'll finish up here and then head out around the park?"

"Sure," he half growled and thought he might have seen her smother a grin. She'd done that a few times and it was pretty enough to distract him from his pain.

Actually, in the few moments when he could focus only on Lacey and forget everything else around them, he didn't much care what she did, as long as she was focused on him, too. He'd had several imaginative thoughts about his pretty photographer in response to the command, "You're waiting for your date. You're anxious for her to arrive. You haven't seen her for a while, and you're thinking about what you'd like to do when she gets here."

He wondered what *she'd* do if she knew what he was thinking he'd like to do to *her.* That he'd like to stretch her out on the blanket he sat on alone, and maybe take some of the honey in the picnic basket and drizzle it over her breasts, sucking the sweetness off the dusky nipples that were just barely visible under the thin cotton of her top. That he'd like to work his way down from there, stripping off those sexy, low-cut army pants she was wearing, and taste the secrets she held between her thighs.

Her camera started making noise, and she smiled. "Oh, that's good, just like that, Jarod," and he nearly exploded with a boner right then. Did she have any idea how sexy she sounded, urging him on, and how she was feeding into his fantasy as if she could read his mind?

Still, there were question marks, he reminded himself, trying to get his desire and his body's response under control. Her rigid body posture when she'd turned, pretending she was taking a phone call. Half of knowing what was coming at you was being able to read body position, expressions…and Lacey had not been happy or relaxed as she had pretended to be when she'd returned. In fact, he'd say whatever she'd picked up on that call had scared her.

Who did she think she was fooling, and why was she trying?

On her signal for a break, he ducked into a small changing station, stripping out of his dress clothes and putting on the designer duds that they provided, surprised when they fit. Thank God they let him keep his boots on.

When he reemerged, he was a little surprised to see the prop guys already throwing their stuff in the back of a small car. The shoot was completely torn down and everyone was leaving. They came over and took down the changing tent almost as soon as he stepped foot out of it. He was glad that they had given him time to get his pants on.

"They're on their way to another shoot, and have to hustle," she said, as if reading his mind. "It's just you and me, now, cowboy."

"What about my clothes?" He looked down at the getup he was in.

"They'll leave them back at the studio, don't worry."

The urban metrosexual look wasn't his usual taste, but he supposed he could live with it for the afternoon. He felt naked without his hat, though, and gazed wistfully at the car that was leaving with his clothes.

"More pictures?" He wasn't sure if he growled, but maybe.

"It will be easy now. You don't have to do anything. I just want some natural shots, nothing formal, so relax. We'll grab a hot dog and enjoy what's left of this gorgeous afternoon, okay? My treat—you were a good sport back there."

"It was easy with you taking the pictures," he said tactfully. It was true in part, because watching her work had been a pleasure. Pure pleasure. "What if I drop mustard on this shirt?"

"You'll owe *Bliss* about fifteen-hundred bucks," she said seriously, making his eyes bulge before she grinned and said, "Gotcha."

He shook his head, laughing, unsure what to make of her. "Does this seriously cost that much? It's just a...*shirt*."

"Yeah, it would go for that much retail, but it's given to *Bliss* so they can use it in shoots. The price is because of the designer's name, and the way it fits, the quality of the material, which is pure silk, by the way. If you could see yourself in it, you'd see how it affects the contours of your body, and even changes the effect when you move, when you walk... That's what people pay big bucks for." She grinned as she watched some women watching him. "That shirt with those jeans makes you sex on legs, cowboy."

"I think I feel objectified," he grumped humorously, but he didn't mind in the least if she wanted to make him into her sex object.

"That's what sexy calendars are all about," she said, laughing. "Though the proceeds from this one will go to a worthy cause, too, so you can take comfort in that."

"It's the only reason I'm here," he said honestly. Well, that and he was under orders to be here.

"I can understand that," she agreed. "For someone who's not used to being in the limelight, and who doesn't look for recognition from his work, this must be kind of awkward, but that's what makes a hero a hero, right? And you guys deserve to be recognized. It's good for people to know there are still heroes in the world, Jarod. People need them."

As they walked underneath a tunnel, he didn't answer, hardly considering himself a hero for doing the job he was trained to do. But was Lacey talking about herself, too? Did she need to believe there were heroes out there? If she knew the thoughts he had about her with her clothes off, she might think him less than heroic.

He was willing to risk it.

As they emerged from the other side of the tunnel under one of the park's many bridges, he saw a yellow ball go rolling across the road. A young girl, no more than four, raced after the ball. Jarod, however, saw the bike rider whipping around the corner toward her, the cyclist hitting his brakes, veering, wheels screeching on the pavement.

Jarod acted on reflex, lunging forward to step in

front of the little girl, her mother calling her name in a panic from the grassy lawn. Jarod scooped the child up, though he couldn't get out of the way fast enough, and the cyclist grazed him as he screeched to a halt, nearly riding into the stone curve of the bridge.

The little girl wiggled in his arms. "My baaaaalllll," she cried, struggling furiously to be let loose.

Jarod set her down, but didn't let go as her mother rushed to them, apologizing, and white as a sheet.

"Delilah! You know better than to ever run off on me like that, ever!" she scolded. The mom's eyes brimmed with tears in delayed reaction to her daughter's close call.

Jarod spotted Lacey talking to the cyclist, and made sure Delilah was firmly attached to her mother before jogging away and retrieving the ball.

"Is he okay?" Jarod asked.

She nodded. "Just shaken up. It was a close call for everyone, but he's fine. You?"

"I'm good," he responded, turning back to give the crying child her toy.

The mother, much calmer, smiled gratefully. "Thank you so much. You could have been hurt, too. You might have saved her life, thank you so much."

Out of habit, he went to touch his hat, but it wasn't there, and he smiled wryly. "No problem, ma'am."

"Play?"

He looked down, and Delilah held her ball up. "Play." She giggled, running off into the grassy lawn, beckoning him.

"Do you mind?" he asked the mom.

"Not in the least. Her dad is in Afghanistan, and I think she misses him playing ball with her. She says he throws it different than I do," the woman said, smiling warmly. Jarod's jaw clenched against the surge of emotion he felt, the respect he couldn't help but feel for the sacrifices others made. He was no hero, not compared to what others were doing in the world.

He was suddenly aware of the whirring sound of the camera, and felt his muscles tighten, then relax again. It was just Lacey doing her thing. He still wasn't used to it.

He caught the ball one last time and brought it to the little girl, smiling. He hoped to hell her dad made it back to play ball with her soon.

"Delilah, I have to go now, but you stay away from the roads, okay? If your ball goes there again, wait for your mom to get it."

She nodded solemnly. "'Kay." She then toddled off to her mother, promptly forgetting him. Jarod returned to where Lacey stood, packing her camera away.

"Done for the day?"

When she looked up, he was caught for a minute by the bare emotion in her eyes. He wasn't sure, but he thought she might have shed a few tears, too.

"Are you okay?" she asked, and her eyes widened, drawing attention to his shirt. "You did get hit. Let me see. Why didn't you say something?"

To be honest, he hadn't even realized it. The shirt hadn't torn but apparently he had picked up a scrape from the bike's handles and there was a small bloody patch on the expensive silk.

"Lacey, I'm sorry—" he started, and then sucked in a breath as she lifted the edge of the material and ran her fingers over the spot where he was injured.

"You should clean this up. It's not deep, but it's bruising."

"Can't even feel it," he said hoarsely, telling the truth, because all he could feel were the cool tips of her fingers on his hot skin. Damn.

She was obviously concerned. So worried about a little scrape, it made him smile.

"Yeah, I'm fine. The shirt's probably ruined, though."

"Who cares about the shirt?"

The vibe between them had changed tangibly as she straightened and they found themselves standing very close. Her expression went from worried to sultry as her eyes drifted to his mouth. The look shot desire through him, and his cock swelled in response—pure male reaction. And if she could do that with just a look, what else could happen between them?

"That was the most amazing thing I ever saw," she said.

"It was just—"

She put a finger to his lips, and the softness of the touch stopped him cold.

"Not 'just' anything. You reacted so fast, without thought. And then playing with that young girl… I don't think I've ever seen anything so brave or so kind in my whole life, Jarod." Her hand moved from where it had been poised on his lips to rub her thumb along his cheek. "You're the real deal, a real hero."

"Lacey," he tried to object again, not wanting her to put him on too high a pedestal, especially with the erection from her touch straining at his jeans. Thank goodness the shirt hung over the front of his pants.

She pushed up on tiptoe and pulled him down as she wrapped her arms around his neck, taking his mouth in a hot and desperate kiss. He responded on instinct, wrapping his arms around her and crushing her up against him.

Her kiss was intense, and her passion equaled his, her tongue rubbing on his invitingly, her hands gripping his back as they strained to be closer than was physically possible.

When giggling cut through the lusty haze of his thoughts, he remembered they were out in the open. As he pulled gently away, he spied a group of teenage girls with knowing eyes, still giggling. He smiled, tilting his forehead against Lacey's, both of them catching their breath.

"That was some kiss," was all he could say.

She laughed, and pressed her lips to his one more time before slipping her hands away to put a few inches between them.

He hadn't seen her glow, not really, until this moment. It was as if a light had turned on inside of her—the sun and the moon and stars all shining through her at once.

"We should go back to your room and wash up that scrape," she said, her voice hitching slightly, her eyes unsure.

He took her hand and brought it to his lips, his own

heart hammering hard as he realized what she was really saying. She didn't have to be unsure with him. He was certain enough for both of them.

"It does sting a bit, now that you mention it."

They walked quickly toward the subway station, their hands mingling, his thumb rubbing the center of her palm.

He let his eyes travel over her body as she stretched upward to grip the handrail. Hanging on, jostling against each other every few seconds, they moved with the sway of the train until it screeched to a halt. He wished he'd brought his handcuffs, imagining her stretched out on a bed like that, her arms secured above her head, while he enjoyed her any way he pleased.

They just about made it inside the apartment before desire exploded between them.

5

LACEY WAS PRETTY SURE she was going to lose her mind by the time he was sliding the small white card into the lock, though she'd been ready for him since they left the park. It had been the longest subway ride of her life. Who knew that a man pressing his thumb to the center of her palm could have her wet and ready so easily?

Jarod was all lean, hard male animal. Pressed up against him, she wound her arms around him, pulling him in, opening her lips and letting him explore to his, and her, delight. She didn't want to think or talk; she wanted to burn the slate of her memories clean and start new right here, right now, with this man.

To move things along, she slid her hands down and around, pressing her palm along the hard ridge between his legs. He moaned his approval, and she reached to undo his belt. She was surprised when he gently nudged her hands away.

"What are you doing?" she asked on a gulp of breath.

"Just slowing us down a little, sweetheart." His gaze burned into hers as he trailed a finger from her cheek to the line of her jaw and shoulder, finally brushing over her left nipple in a touch that made her catch her breath. "I plan to take my time and enjoy you."

She shook her head. "Fast the first time. Then slow after that. Please, just fuck me," she said on a quivering breath, holding his gaze.

She didn't want to tell him that slow would give her too much time to think. Even now, she was afraid that if she stopped looking at him, if he stopped touching her for too long, the chill would settle in when all she wanted was his heat.

She held her breath as they shared a silent look for several heartbeats, and when he moved his hands down to his belt, loosening it, she almost thanked the heavens aloud.

It only took her a minute to catch up, stripping off her clothes, and then they were both naked and wrapped around each other, just as she'd hoped they would be.

The branding of his hot flesh on hers was a welcome mark she'd never forget. She pressed in, wanting it all, touching gently, cupping his balls in her hand, squeezing in a way that pulled a moan from deep inside of him.

She smiled into the kiss as she stroked his rock-hard shaft, rolling her thumb over the head and feeling him shudder. He filled her hand, and she wanted him filling *her*. The thought of him inside her had her muscles aching and clenching, begging for contact after having been empty for so long.

His hands palmed her breasts, alternately rubbing and pinching her nipples.

She levered herself up to slide her legs around his hips, and in turn he slid his hands around her backside to lift her as he carried her, never breaking their kiss until he had to speak.

"Protection," he said, nodding toward his suitcase on the chair and setting her down long enough to search inside.

She drank the sight of him in, all taut muscle and golden skin. Later, she'd have to ask him why, exactly, he didn't show any tan lines. He leaned down and grabbed a box from the suitcase. A big box.

She smiled. "You thought ahead. Figured a cowboy might get lucky in the big city?"

The look he shot her direction was pure sex. "I never could have imagined getting *this* lucky," he said, sweeping a look down over her body and back to her face. "You're perfect," he said roughly.

She blushed from the intensity of his inspection, watching him as he slipped the transparent latex over a very lovely, thick erection. She might have licked her lips.

"I need you," she whispered, walking to him, needing to finish what they started. "Now."

"You've got me." He pulled her into his arms. Wasting no time finding her core, he slid deep inside, one sure thrust linking them together, chasing her demons away. He swallowed her gasp and moved them to a spot where nothing hung on the wall, pushing her up against it.

"Hang on, honey," he warned on a raspy breath, making her laugh even as her entire body seemed to clutch in ecstasy.

Oh, how she'd missed this. She tried to hold on to all the sensations assaulting her, to the feeling of being completely connected to someone, to all this raw male power throbbing inside of her. Soon, though, there was too much, and she gave herself over. Jarod braced her against the wall and thrust into her, hard and fast, just as she'd asked for. Her mind blanked completely.

Yes.

"More, more, more, harder, *please*." She wasn't sure if she was begging or demanding as she chanted in time with the staccato rhythm of his thrusts. Her body stretched and expanded to accommodate him as he seemed to push even deeper, touching her where no one had ever touched, taking her places she hadn't been.

Big, sure hands cupped her bottom, holding her in place firmly, and she cried out when his fingertips brushed over the sensitive bud between her cheeks, igniting a hard climax so unexpected that she felt tears on her cheeks as the sweetness of it claimed her.

When she opened her eyes, it was to find him watching her, his face close to hers, features taut, irises dilated. He was wild and yet completely in control. She could probably ask him to stop right now, and somehow, she knew he would.

Her muscles tightened around him as he seemed to get even thicker and heavier inside of her, and she knew he was probably close. His breath was labored, his back turning rock-hard under her fingers.

"I want you to come with me, darlin'."

"I don't know if I can again. That was so good," she said on a half gasp, half laugh.

Something primal and deliberate gleamed in his eyes, and she knew her admission had been received as a challenge. It made her shiver.

"I think we can do better," he said, teasing, but sounding completely serious all the same.

She squeaked as he pushed her legs up higher, his hips widening the space between her legs. He opened her completely and pushed the velvety hardness of his pelvis fully against the soft folds of her sex.

He literally touched her everywhere, inside and out, and she dug her nails into his shoulder blades reflexively. Her head fell forward from the onslaught of pleasure, seeking more. She couldn't move, literally pinned against the wall, but he was moving in all the right ways.

"That's it, sweetheart," he crooned as his chest rubbed against her breasts, as the hard muscle of his abdomen ground against her clit relentlessly. She took her hands from his shoulders and pushed her breasts together, letting him suck both nipples simultaneously, a move that had her spiraling out of control.

Within seconds, she felt him shudder and buck against her while she melted in his arms, coming apart so completely she lost all sense of where she was. For several long moments there was nothing except for heat, waves of pulsating pleasure and Jarod.

They stayed together against the wall, catching their breath and coming back down. When she felt him move, felt his body leave hers, he didn't put her down on the floor. Instead, he flipped her around easily and carried her with him to the bed. Laying her down and moving over her, he stretched out beside her and pulled her onto his chest.

The protective, gentle gesture moved her and tears threatened again for very different reasons. When one slipped down and splashed on his chest, he pulled back, looking at her in concern.

"Hey, you okay?" he asked, studying her intently. But the panic or discomfort she was accustomed to seeing when men were faced with women's tears was absent. He was too much man to be scared by tears.

She nodded, smiling, crying, and feeling like a complete, naked idiot.

"I'm good…better than good. It's just that was so good, and you're so…nice," she said lamely. The emotions she was experiencing defied words.

"It was good," he agreed easily, still watching her. "And you're pretty easy to be nice to, Lacey."

She didn't know what to say and buried her face in his chest again, loving the texture of his skin, how he smelled and how fantastic he felt, too.

"Hey, we forgot to fix up your scrape," she said softly.

"We can do that later. I think it's okay," he replied and she could hear the smile in his voice.

He mindlessly stroked her arm, and then brought her fingers up to his mouth for a kiss, and she sighed in bliss. Anxiety and tears disappeared in a relaxed afterglow that she hadn't felt for ages. Though really, had she ever felt this? This exact combination of satisfaction, warmth and ease? It was as close to heaven as she could imagine.

"What's this?" he asked, and she realized he'd been inspecting the arm he'd been kissing. She'd completely forgotten the scars there. Reality crashed in hard, and she yanked her arm back.

"Nothing. Just an old injury."

"Not that old."

She looked at him apprehensively. He read the question in her eyes and answered simply, "I have a few scars of my own, and I've seen plenty more. Those seem pretty recent. How does a photographer end up with that many stitches?"

She had to think fast, and shrugged, hoping she sounded casual. "I fell in my bathtub about a year ago. Broke my arm, and sliced that part below the elbow on the faucet."

"Sounds bad."

"It wasn't fun, but it's healed now," she said easily, amazed at how the lie fell out, and not liking that she'd become used to hiding the truth. But it was about survival and privacy. She was entitled.

She certainly didn't feel threatened by Jarod. She wouldn't be here with him if she did, but no way would she tell him the truth. Especially now—he'd never look at her the same way if he knew. She'd found out quickly that once you admitted to being a victim, people changed how they saw you, and not for the better. So she simply wouldn't admit it.

"Good thing, since you're going to need every bit of strength you have," he said, kissing her hair. He then moved out from beneath her, letting her slip onto the pile of pillows. He was, truly, the most handsome man she'd ever laid eyes on, and even more so here in his naked, tousled, sleepy-eyed state. She pushed up on one elbow when he shifted from the mattress, and leaned over to pick up her camera bag.

"What are you doing?"

"How complicated is this camera to operate?"

"Not bad. I mean, it's up to the photographer to know how to take a good picture. The camera is just a tool."

His eyes remained on hers steadily. "Could I handle it?"

It took her a minute before what he was suggesting landed in her mind, and she felt herself physically pull back.

"I'm sure you could, but we're not going there," she said definitively.

His eyebrows quirked up. "Why not? You've had this thing trained on me all day, even when I wasn't aware of it. Don't you think turnaround is fair play?"

"You weren't naked. It wasn't sex."

"I felt more exposed than that, at some points," he confessed.

She blinked. "Why?"

"I'm not used to being watched like that. I don't know what you're homing in on. What you're seeing. You're in complete control."

Settling into the pillows, she had to admit that she'd never thought about it that way. Most of the subjects she'd shot were models, and were used to being in the limelight. She hadn't considered how vulnerable it could make someone, like Jarod, feel—a man who was always used to being in control.

"Okay, I get that, but this is different."

"How? It's another way I can get to know you…and it's your camera, your film. You can just destroy it later if you want to. Though I'd love to see the photos first," he added in a voice like warm honey.

Like many photographers, Lacey preferred being on the working end of the camera for a reason, but she had to admit, the look on Jarod's face was compelling. And the idea of giving him that gift was seductive.

She smiled. "What if you don't like what you see?"

He shook his head resolutely. "No chance of that," he promised, his eyes drifting over her as she lounged on the bed.

She paused, considering. He'd let her demand what she wanted earlier, given her what she needed without holding back. He had only showed her passion, consideration, kindness. She knew if she told him no, he'd listen.

So maybe it was a moment for her to give him something.

"Okay, there's only a dozen or so pictures left on there anyway, but let me show you what to do."

Heat and something else—admiration?—flared in his eyes when she agreed. Her own breath became a little short at the thought of what they were about to do.

After a few quick instructions, she wasn't sure if she was more nervous about being photographed nude or him handling her expensive camera. But his hands were sure, and he took a position at the end of the bed.

As he lifted the camera to his eye, she froze for a second, wondering what to do. The barrel of the lens seemed to zero in on her, tagging her to the spot. She'd never realized how it felt to be so tightly zoomed in on, explored—exposed.

But her frozen posture gave way to heat as he spoke.

"Relax on those pillows…think about what we did a few minutes ago. Think about me inside of you, fucking you up against the wall."

How did he know so easily what to say, what turned her on? She loved sex talk, hard, raw and honest. It was how she liked sex, as well, and Jarod seemed of a like mind.

"Open up your legs…let me see what you're hiding there," he continued playfully, his tone light and teasing, and she did as he asked.

She dealt with her nerves by hamming it up at first, mocking a sexy pose against the pillows, letting her thighs fall only so far apart, teasing, and lifting her arms up to jut her breasts out for his view. She imagined she looked ridiculous. She was confident in her body, but wasn't built to pull off the sexy poses her more voluptuous models could. She was more…made for modeling running clothes or sports equipment.

When she heard him suck in a breath, bite off a short curse and saw his cock spring forward with interest as he took the shot, she reconsidered. Doing what he said, she looked over at the spot where he'd held her against the wall, buried inside of her, and pushed up on all fours, looking back at him over her shoulder. The click of the camera and his harsh breathing egged her on.

"You're so incredibly hot," he said, his voice rough,

telling her he was not unaffected. "Touch yourself for me."

The lens connected them; model and photographer were always linked in an intimate way, even more so in this kind of situation. She did as he asked, catching her breath as her hand slipped between her legs and found her skin sensitive and soft. She knew how to make herself feel good, and didn't hold back. Hearing the soft hum of the zoom focusing, she knew he was making it a tighter shot. As liquid warmth seemed to move through her limbs, she lost her self-consciousness and let her eyes rest on his sex. It was perfectly built, like the rest of him, and it strained toward her.

"You have the most beautiful cock. I want to suck you," she said softly, trembling as her own touch brought her to the edge.

"I'd love to see that, Lacey. I want to see your mouth moving on me, making me come," he growled as he took the shot, and his words, the image they built in her mind, pushed gentle cries of pleasure past her lips.

She opened her eyes as he set the camera on the dresser and turned to her, his body set in rigid, sensual tension.

"Can we set this on remote?"

She told him how and a minute or two later he was back on the bed with her, the camera watching them from its lonely post on the dresser. As he moved down, stretching out at her side, she was moved by the dark emotion, the passion and the need in his expression.

"Thank you for sharing this with me, for being so open with me," he said simply, his fingers stroking the inside of her thigh.

"It was…intense," she said, propping up on one elbow and meeting his eyes for a moment before she shimmied down and closed her lips over his cock, sucking off the dew there. She moaned in soft approval as he lay back, arching up into her mouth.

She reached over and hit the remote snap without looking.

"I want to taste you, too," he whispered, and she swung her legs over, straddling him as she explored his sex with her mouth. He broke her concentration, opening her with his hands and prodding her clit more insistently with this tongue.

Gasping, she forgot all about the camera, following the steady current of pleasure that his strokes created, making her crazy with the tricks of his fingers and the talent of his mouth. It became a game between them. He would find a way to drive her one bit further, and then she would go down deeper, suck harder, find a sensitive spot with her tongue, until they were both convulsing with the pleasure of mutual victory.

She pushed back on the pillows, and he followed, sinking down next to her.

She brushed her fingers tenderly over his onyx hair, silently drawing his attention upward to the camera.

Her head rested in the crook of his shoulder, his arms around her, one finding its way up into her hair, holding her head against him in a gesture so intimate she thought she wouldn't be able to breathe. They lay there, snuggling quietly, replete for the moment.

Spotting the remote on the mattress where she'd

dropped it, she reached it without moving, and with a lazy, satisfied smile, she stopped time with a press of her finger, capturing them both.

6

LACEY WALKED BACK to her apartment feeling loose and well exercised—and she was smiling. Considering they hadn't slept more than a couple of hours combined, she should be worried about her model having rings under his eyes and her ability to stay awake, and…she wasn't worried about any of it. She could barely keep herself from grinning ear to ear.

She felt like her old self again, and it was wonderful.

Jarod was wonderful, too. Considerate, adventurous…and with stamina women dreamed about. She didn't know if they'd continue to spend their nights together, but she also wasn't sure how she'd be able to function if she didn't have a way to deal with the inevitable turn-on of working with him. Incredibly, after everything they'd done, she wanted more. The very idea of looking at him through a camera made her lick her lips.

And today was beach day. He'd be taking off his shirt, and she couldn't wait. Fortunately it was minimal crew, wardrobe was simple and the formal part of the day wouldn't take long. He'd seemed agreeable with the same schedule as before—do the staged shoots, then move around the area taking some candids.

Of course, she thought, placing her hand over the spot in her camera bag where she kept her film, nothing quite as candid as the shots they'd taken last night.

Would she develop them?

She grinned more widely. Life was good. Lacey hummed to herself as she turned up the steps to her apartment, taking the stairs and doing a little jog all the way down the hall. She was running a bit late, and had to—

Stopping in her tracks, she noticed the door was open. Just a crack, but it was open. She tried not to panic as her heart began to hammer and she fumbled reaching for her cell phone.

She suddenly understood why the seemingly stupid heroines always rushed in to the house when they knew there was danger waiting inside—she had to make herself step back, remembering the general advice to call police in such a situation, not rush in.

But underneath the fear was anger. Someone had intruded in her space, in her world. She wanted desperately to burst through the door and answer the question *who*. To stop it, to know why.

The driving need to know nearly pushed her into the apartment, regardless of the danger that was possibly inside.

Instead, she dialed 911 and waited, reported the break-in, and moved back down to the stairway, never taking her eyes off the door, even though the operator had told her to meet the police at the entry. She was determined to know if someone came out of her place.

Nothing happened. The hall was silent, and she didn't hear anything coming from the room, either. Her neighbors were mostly professionals like herself and had likely left for work. She was alone.

Doubt wheedled itself into the cracks of her panicked thoughts. Had she forgotten to lock the apartment? Could her super have gone in for some reason and failed to shut the door completely?

Too late for second guesses as she heard the police come through the door downstairs. She looked at them in both relief and worry as they climbed the stairs toward her.

"You reported a break-in, ma'am?" one guy who could have been a candidate for the calendar asked her.

"Yes, I mean, I don't know, but the door was open, and I'm sure I locked it, but I—"

"You stay right here. You did the right thing by not going in. Let us check it out. I'd recommend you go outside just in case."

Lacey nodded, although she didn't actually go anywhere. Her feet seemed to be frozen to the spot as the two officers moved carefully down the hall toward her apartment, standing at each side, covering each other as they nudged the door open, and went in.

Nothing.

Lacey didn't realize she was holding her breath until she let it go when one of the policemen came out and waved her down the hall toward the apartment.

"You can come in now, ma'am, but I have to warn you, it's a shock. Someone was here," he said with a stern expression. She walked past him, wanting to know what on earth he was talking about. Then she stopped cold in her doorway, sucking in a breath, her world tilting a little.

"Oh, my God…"

Everything was a wreck. The entire contents of her apartment had been upended, and whoever it was had written *BITCH* in huge black letters with spray paint across one wall, where she was sure to see it first thing through the door.

"Lacey, what…what the *hell?*"

She jumped as she recognized Jarod's voice beside her and faced off with him. The adrenaline was pushing through her system so violently she didn't know where to aim her anger first. He grabbed her by the shoulders, leveling her a look.

"What happened here? Are you okay?"

She wrestled away. Her breath coming harshly, she eyed him warily. "How did you know where I live?"

It was impossible for her to separate all of the conflicting emotions coursing through her at the moment, so she targeted them all in his direction. The cop stepped forward, not quite between her and Jarod, but almost.

"Step back, sir," he said in warning. Jarod nodded, stepping back, but only slightly.

"I'm just…a concerned friend," Jarod explained, "You can pull my wallet—and my badge—from my left pocket. I'm a cop, too. Texas Ranger, El Paso."

The second officer joined them to see what the fuss was about, and Lacey's mind cleared. She started to tell them that Jarod wasn't the one she was worried about just as they took his wallet and flipped open his badge.

"Ranger, huh? Well, you aren't from around here, and the lady doesn't seem happy to see you, so maybe we should walk you out."

Jarod looked at her, making her look at him.

"Is that what you want, Lacey? You want me to leave?"

Lacey didn't know what to think, but casting a glance at her apartment, she shook her head.

"No, I want you to stay. I'm sorry, officers, I…was shocked," she finished lamely, and the NYPD men watched her carefully for a few moments before finally relenting.

"I'll call this in and we'll need a report," one said, and they all nodded, flanking Lacey as they walked deeper into the apartment. Jarod was closest to her. She welcomed his presence as much as she questioned it. She knew he couldn't be responsible for this, but how he showed up when he did, and how he found her address…they'd talk about that before this was over.

As she scanned the mess in her apartment, she reached for something to hang on to and Jarod's firm, warm grip was there. When she turned into his chest, he was there. It gave her the strength she needed to turn back around and face what she had to.

"Have you received any threats lately, Ms. Graham? We would chalk it up to breaking and entering, but this—" the cop's eyes traveled to the scrawl "—seems pretty directed. Personal. And it doesn't look like the usual stuff was taken. Your television, even your laptop, is still here."

"I—I can't imagine who would do this," she said, though she didn't meet their eyes.

She'd call Gena, the secretary from Legal Aid, and find out what was going on, if Scott was where he was supposed to be. But who else would have done something like this? The police were right. There wasn't anything missing, although several things were broken. The break-in was definitely a message of some sort.

"Or they were searching for something, and it wasn't here," Jarod offered reasonably.

"I can't imagine what," she responded as the officers took notes.

"You didn't spend the night here, last night, Ms. Graham. Did anyone know that?"

"No, it was…a last-minute decision." Her cheeks flamed and she refused to look at Jarod.

"It's just as well you weren't here, but did you have anything with you that the intruder might have been looking for?"

She shook her head. "All I had was my camera bag, my film, my lenses…undeveloped shots from the past few days. Nothing anyone would want."

"Hard to say. What kinds of photos?"

Her cheeks turned hotter as this time she did meet Jarod's gaze, thinking of their private photo session. "They're modeling shots for *Bliss Magazine*. That's it…"

"Maybe someone was up to something they shouldn't have been, and you caught it on film," the other officer speculated, and Lacey blinked. Did things like that happen in real life? Could she have gathered some kind of evidence against someone in the park or in her candids that they'd later come looking for?

"Well, the pictures aren't developed yet, and I'll check through them carefully, but how would some stranger know I took the picture, or where I lived?"

Jarod nodded in agreement. "And why the message? Why go to the trouble? They'd want to get in, get the film, and get out—ideally without being seen or noticed."

"True," the officer agreed. "Well, then, as nothing was stolen and no other harm was done, I guess that's all we can do here. But if you have any more trouble, be sure to call us," he said.

"Thank you, I will." Lacey closed the door behind them, and turned toward her apartment again, the day shot down the tubes. She'd had to cancel the session, and now she had to deal with this mess.

"So do you want to tell me what's going on?" Jarod asked calmly, standing in the middle of her living room, looking big and imposing among the disaster, looking at her as if he could see right through her.

"Excuse me?"

"Listen, Lacey, normally I mind my own business, but you've been as jumpy as a jackrabbit since I laid eyes on you, and now this? I saw your face when he asked you if you'd had any problems recently. You're not as good a liar as you think you are. Who's bothering you? Why would they do *this?*"

She stepped forward, eyes blazing as her heart thudded in her chest. He was too close, and she pushed back, hard.

"It's really none of your business! Just because we had sex it's not an invitation into my life. How did you show up here anyway? You've never come to my apartment, you couldn't possibly know where I lived unless you…" The answer dawned, and she put her hand to the edge of a table near the door to steady herself. "You've been following me?"

The sick feeling in the pit of her stomach increased as she saw the truth on his face, and she didn't bother holding back tears, but they were mostly from anger at herself, for being so stupid as to let her guard down. Thank God she had the pictures, she realized. Regret was a second blow, and she leaned harder on the edge of the table for support.

"Just get out before I call the police back. Forget about the shoot, leave me alone. I mean it."

For a second, they were both still, and she didn't know what was going to happen. He didn't seem angry; he didn't step forward. When he spoke, she could hardly believe her ears.

"Sorry, darlin', but that just isn't happening until you tell me what's going on."

JAROD FELT as if he'd already stepped over a line, but there was no way he was going anywhere. Lacey was in trouble, and he wanted to know the source of it. He wanted to help.

He'd do anything for this woman. He didn't know how he knew that, but he knew. In the same way he knew she was wounded, and frightened of something she was too stubborn to admit.

"Lacey, listen for a moment."

She started to protest, her eyes wild, arms wrapped

so tightly around her slim frame that he had to hold himself back from going to her and holding her himself. But now wasn't the time for that.

"I did follow you, but not to scare you. I... Oh, hell," he cursed, throwing his hands up. "I like you. I really like you, but there's been something going on here. I can see the fear on your face, the way you react to things like a sudden movement or someone crowding your space. It's as if you're poised to run. People don't normally react that way unless they've been given a reason to."

She looked away, and he knew he'd hit on the truth. But could he convince her to share? To trust?

"Then there was that phone call, and now this. I'm not stupid, Lacey. I knew something spooked you the other day, and so I simply followed you back to your apartment so I could make sure you got there safely. That's all. Then today, I saw the cops arrive, and I lost it. I had to make sure you were okay.

"Lacey, I hope you know I'd never hurt you—not a hair on your head. Not after what we shared, and I, well..." He blew out an exasperated breath, unfamiliar and uneasy with sharing his thoughts this way. "I hope you wouldn't have slept with me in the first place if you thought you couldn't trust me. I'm sorry if following you scared you. That's the last thing I would ever do."

She didn't say anything, but he could see her processing the information. He took a step closer, then another, until he was standing beside her, and lifted his hand to brush some of the hair from her eyes. Hell, the worst she could do was hit him and tell him to leave again, but the fight seemed to have gone out of her.

He wasn't sure if that was a good thing or not.

"Lacey—" he started, but she didn't say anything; pressed her fingers to his lips, silencing him.

"I believe you, Jarod, and I guess I have been jumpy. I just never expected anything like this," she whispered, looking around at the apartment.

He closed his eyes, relieved about her accepting his apology.

"I know, and I'll help you clean up. I'd like it if you'd stay with me again tonight, at my hotel." He said the words on a smoky note as her form pressed against his. Protectiveness wasn't the only thing he was feeling for this woman.

"No, I won't be driven out of my own apartment. They probably won't even come back."

"They?"

She shook her head. "Generic pronoun. I don't know who it is, I really don't. I did get a weird call, and sometimes I have the feeling someone is watching me, but I thought that was my imagination."

"This isn't imaginary."

"I know. Jarod, I have to make another phone call. Privately," she said, and he nodded. She still wasn't telling him what was going on, but this wasn't a time to push.

"Sure, I'll go check out your kitchen and start setting things to rights."

"You don't have to do that," she protested.

"I want to. I want to be here, with you, Lacey. Okay?"

She almost smiled, and seemed to relax slightly, and Jarod did, too. He walked through louvered French doors to the kitchen and was tempted to hang close, but he said he'd give her privacy, and he did.

The kitchen was less untidy. He picked up the garbage, and straightened out a few other things, listening to Lacey's voice as she spoke to someone in low tones, although he couldn't make out the words.

As he put the garbage pail back in the corner, his eye caught sight of a crunched sheet of paper on top. He couldn't help but see the name underneath the letterhead, "Domestic Abuse Counseling."

The scar on Lacey's arm, the way she'd panicked when the CHIP guy had gotten too aggressive… An ugly picture was forming in his mind. Yet, this could be junk mail and have nothing to do with her at all.

As his fingers touched the edges, he hesitated again. No.

If Lacey had been abused, if she had one man violating her life, he wouldn't be another one, no matter how much he wanted to know.

It was up to her to tell him about her past if she wanted to, if she could trust him enough. He pushed the paper back down into the garbage and turned away.

But in his heart, the details had started to form a truth he hadn't really considered. The protectiveness he'd felt before blossomed into something much, much more powerful.

When Lacey walked in, he'd just dumped a dustpan of broken glass into the garbage pail and had the place almost looking normal again. She seemed relieved.

Whether it was finding the kitchen not as wrecked as the living room, or the phone calls she'd made, the color was back in her cheeks, her eyes were less panicked.

"I'm sorry that took so long, I just had to check on something."

Like an ex-spouse or boyfriend?

"No problem. Apparently the kitchen wasn't a huge draw for your intruder—not so bad in here."

"Thank you, Jarod, and thanks for staying. I know I…reacted badly to you showing up, but I'm really glad you're here."

He took a deep breath. It was something. More than he'd expected, maybe more than he deserved, considering the circumstances.

"I'm glad I'm here, too," he said, smiling. Crossing the kitchen to pull her close, he was happy when she came willingly into his arms. "I thought I'd go get some paint and take care of your wall art in there. Any color you like in particular? New paint job? I don't offer often, so take advantage," he teased, rubbing his hands over her back, and feeling her body expand and contract with a sigh.

"You definitely don't have to do that. Seriously. The super will send someone to take care of it," she said, leaning back and looking up. "But thanks."

"I don't want you having to see it one minute longer than you have to. I don't mind," he insisted, liking how when she leaned back from him their hips met, his groin snuggling against hers.

"I guess I would be a fool to turn down more help."

"Let's put things to rights, and then I'm taking you to dinner. If the day is lost for work, we might as well find some small enjoyment in the meantime, huh?"

"Sounds like a plan."

They worked in tandem for several hours, and before long, the apartment was put back together again. Still, it bothered him to see her so controlled, so measured, as she picked up broken objects that were obviously important to her, and put them in the garbage. She didn't cry once, but repressed emotion strained every muscle in her lithe body, and he knew from his own experience the mental and physical toll something like this took.

Jarod didn't plan to leave her alone. If she wouldn't stay with him, he'd find a way to convince her he should stay here. Admiring the pout of pretty breasts under her T-shirt and remembering how her soft skin tasted, he didn't think it would be a sacrifice.

"There. Not bad," she announced, gesturing at her room, studiously avoiding the wall where the first coat of paint was drying. He'd used a stain-blocker, but the black was tough to cover against a light wall, and it still showed slightly. He would put on the second coat in a few hours.

Jarod walked up behind her, massaging her neck, playing along. Sometimes it was necessary to just act normally even when things obviously weren't normal at all.

She turned, and he was leveled by the emotion in her eyes when she looked up at him.

"Thank you, Jarod," she said simply.

He felt like the richest man on earth. *I am in so much*

trouble with this woman, he thought, as he leaned down to kiss her, wondering how he'd gotten in so deep, so fast.

7

OVER STEAMING PLATES of Chinese food at a tiny place downtown, Lacey laughed hysterically as she watched Jarod, one of the most capable men she could imagine, fumble with chopsticks until he finally gave up and signaled the waiter for a fork.

"The food smells great. I'd actually like to eat some of it," he said, smiling at the waiter who offered him utensils. "I don't know how you manage those things," he said, eyeing her chopsticks with malice.

She wiggled her fingers at him after popping a succulent straw mushroom into her mouth.

"Nimble fingers, I guess," she replied.

He snatched the fingers of her other hand gently and brought them to his mouth. "Don't I know it."

Heat shot up her arm and swept away any other thought. In fact, though this had been close to one of her top-ten worst days ever, in the past half hour she hadn't even thought about her apartment. Sitting here amid the colorful sights and sounds of the bustling neighborhood, she sighed, actually feeling happy.

It was completely incongruous. How could she be *happy* when she'd just suffered a break-in, and Scott was out of jail? Not that the two were connected, but they could be. Who else would do this to her? Who else would make it so personal?

"Hey. What's going on in there?" Jarod asked, a concerned expression on his face.

"Just thinking how nice it is to sit here and forget everything, which of course made me remember it all."

He reached over, and squeezed her hand. "I'm here if you want to talk about it, and even if you don't."

She smiled, grateful, but apprehensive. Whatever it was between them had the telltale signs of turning into something far more complicated than a fling, and that worried her. It was too fast, for one thing, and he was going back home soon, for another.

Sleeping with a guy for some mutual fun, fine— starting a relationship with him—that she wasn't sure she was ready for. Jarod was incredible, but the way he was getting so close was making her uncomfortable, so she went to a more comfortable topic: work.

"Listen, we have to make up the beach shots in studio, which should take a day, and then another day around the city. We're scheduled for the Empire State Building tomorrow, so we could wrap this up sooner than we thought. You could probably be back tracking down bad guys in Texas by next week."

His eyes narrowed. "Really? Well…that's good to know, I guess."

"Yes, I'm sure you want to get back."

"That was before—"

He was cut off by the ringing of his cell, and she tried to hold off a visible sigh of relief. The call must not have been good news, though, but she couldn't tell much from his regular nods and grunts of acknowledgment to someone named Tom.

"No problem, Tom. I'll go now."

He hung up, but something had changed. The lines of his face seemed harder drawn, and he didn't look at her, not right away.

"Is everything okay?"

"That was my captain. There's a guy we've been tracking—bad case—and he jumped bail a few days ago. A small-town policeman just north of here grabbed someone on a DWI with the same name, and they want me to check if it's him, and if so, send him home. I may have to go with him."

Her eyes widened. "But the calendar!"

He blinked, and she wasn't sure if she saw disappointment flash across his face. She felt like an ass. He'd been so good to her, and all she could think about was her work. Talk about messed up. She was definitely not in shape for a relationship, and she grimaced. He replied calmly, but set down his fork.

"Let me see what the story is. It might not even be him, but we have to make sure. This is important."

She couldn't help feeling stung at that. "This job is important, as well."

"We're talking about a guy who kills people. And technically, while I'm up here on the department's request, I'm not on vacation. If they tell me to do something, it has to take precedence."

She knew he was right. Obviously tracking down a felon was more important than a magazine's calendar, but disappointment stabbed at her, as well, and that was not a good sign. She didn't want him to leave, but there was no way she could admit that.

She nodded. "Sorry, that was uncalled-for. I know you have to do this. It's been one thing after another with this shoot, and just…life. We can reschedule. It's not like we haven't been jostling everything around lately anyway."

She signaled for the check, feeling like an idiot— when had she ever been this needy or this stupid?

"Lacey," Jarod began, but paused as he took the bill from the waiter, though she'd grabbed for it first. "This isn't just work, and it's on me."

"Uh, sure. Okay."

She felt awkward and restless, and just wanted to get out of the restaurant.

"I'll be back by morning if I can. Will you be okay?"

"Sure. I'll try to get one of the local guys for the sky-scraper shots, and—"

"I didn't mean will the shoot work out. I meant will *you* be okay?"

She swallowed. "I'm fine. In fact, I'm going to head to the studio now and make up for some lost time."

He frowned. "Tonight?"

"I often work late into the night. It's not unusual for us artsy types," she said lightly, but secretly the real truth was that she couldn't go back to her apartment. Not yet. Not at night, alone.

"I'll walk you there."

"Not necessary. Really, go. I'm fine," she stressed again.

"It will make me feel better to walk you to the studio."

She paused. She hadn't considered that he could be worried, too. He shouldn't be worried. She didn't want that. His concern for her triggered guilt about her lack of honesty concerning her past, and Scott, but she also couldn't help the relief she felt at Jarod's insistence.

She didn't tell anyone about Scott, and Jarod wasn't the exception to that rule. She didn't want ugliness from her past coloring what she was enjoying with him. They were having fun together, everything was good, and if it would make him feel better to make sure she was safe, what was the harm? It would give her a few more minutes of his company, too.

"That would be nice, thanks," she acknowledged, and they fell into step together, heading to the subway. "We'll catch a train and it won't take long."

As he grabbed her arm, she felt herself spun around in front of him, and gasped in surprise. He pulled her up tight against him, the granite planes of his chest feeling all-too-good. They ignored a few wolf whistles and comments by passersby as he leaned in and kissed her in a way that assured her he wasn't entirely in a hurry.

"I don't want you feeling pressured, but I like you," he said once he broke the kiss, getting right to the point. "I *really* like you. I don't know what that means, but let's not rush to the end of this, okay?"

He didn't give her a chance to answer. Instead, he wound his hand in her hair and tilted her head back so that her breasts pressed into his chest. Her nipples sensitized and peaked as arousal coursed through her. His tongue rubbed against hers in a lazy, mating motion that reminded her what it was like when he was inside of her.

When he released her and looked down askance, all she could do was whisper, "Okay."

He smiled, and her knees went a little weak. She'd yell at herself for being such a sap later. Right now, all she wanted was for him to go, come back, and kiss her again.

PARANOID ABOUT leaving anything at her apartment, she'd dragged her camera bag along with her to dinner, and that included the roll of film containing the pictures of her and Jarod from the hotel.

Soon, she was lost in her own world, ensconced in the basement labs of the *Bliss* building. The rooms were still functional, though not used as much as they used to be now that everything was going digital. It made her sad. She was a romantic at heart, and she loved the tangible experience of bringing a photograph to life.

The photos she was working on now had nothing to do with her project, though. She watched with an analytical eye as the first image came forward, Jarod's strong features slowly emerging, and her jaw dropped as she saw what he'd photographed. There were some ultrasexy shots of herself that had made her chuckle, slightly embarrassed but privately pleased at how he'd viewed her through the camera. Then she came to the images of them together.

As a photographer, she was impressed, and couldn't

ignore the chemistry leaping from the images of them. As a woman, she…she wasn't sure what she felt as she took in Jarod with his face turned into her thigh, looking for all the world as if he was worshipping her, his eyes shuttered, his concentration complete.

A thrill shimmied its way through to her core, making her inner muscles heat and clench as she remembered what it was like as he had slowly made his way upward, to fasten those amazing lips on her clit and suck her into sheer oblivion. And how she'd returned the favor.

Her heart hammered as she revealed one shot after another documenting the progress of the raw desire between them. When she reached the final shot, the one of them cuddled together afterward, their arms wrapped around each other, faces mirroring the satisfaction of the climax they'd just shared, something settled deep inside her heart.

This was not just any man. Not a fling. The images revealed so much more than that.

Her hands shook as she hung the prints to dry, her eyes following the photo story of their lovemaking from start to finish.

She noticed she was rubbing her arm as she admired the photos. He didn't know about her past. Maybe he suspected, but he didn't know. Would it change how he looked at her? Shouldn't she give him more credit? He was obviously an extraordinary man.

He hadn't called yet. Would he be back in the morning, or off to Texas, leaving her in the lurch? Jackie's message had said that Mr. July was out, having suffered a serious injury in the line of duty. Now they might be losing another model, or at least having the schedule disrupted. Mr. April, however, of the FDNY, would be coming in to take Jarod's place for the day, so at least she'd get something done.

Lacey had to wait for the prints to dry before she could leave. Very likely no one used these darkrooms much any more, but she couldn't take a chance with material that was so personal.

Her eyes were tired, and there was a cot in the corner. More than one magazine photog had put in long hours here in the past.

Several hours later, a noise pulled her sharply from her sleep, and she sat up, her heart beating hard. She was momentarily disoriented. Something was wrong.

Gathering her wits, she realized what it was in a flash of shock—the pictures. None of them were hanging where she'd left them. Unbidden panic burbled in her chest as she heard a shuffling noise by the door and she stood on shaky legs, trying to cross the room quietly, grabbing a jar of developing chemicals, the only weapon available to her.

"Who's there? I've called the police," she warned loudly, grabbing her cell phone from her pocket, but grimacing when she saw she had no signal down here.

"Too late. Time for payback, bitch," a sneering and definitely male voice said; though it was muffled through the door, hard to recognize, the sentiment was clear.

She knew what had happened as she heard the man laugh, and footsteps walking away. Whoever it was must have followed her from the restaurant, but how could he have gotten inside the building? He was leaving—with her pictures!

"Oh, no, you aren't," she said with a burst of determination—she couldn't stand the idea of someone else having those pictures. It could ruin her career, or Jarod's.

She grabbed the door handle, feeling the heat building up on the other side. An acrid smell assaulted her, and her heart sank in fear.

Fire.

She couldn't see anything, the room was locked and tightly scaled against light, but some smoke was finding its way under the door. She was trapped.

It had to be Scott.

She fought to keep her breathing steady, her mind clear as the room seemed to close in around her.

Options?

She took a blanket from the cot and jammed it into the crack under the door, stemming the progress of the smoke. She pulled her shirt up over her face, and hit the hard door, yelling, "Help! I'm in here!"

Someone had to hear—they had to.

She looked at her watch. The sun was coming up, and there would be people arriving for work. She heard the fire alarm ring, and relief washed through her. Help would come; she just had to sit tight.

Easier said than done, she thought, pacing. Smoke was filtering in, and she had to get out, soon. Taking a breath, she started banging on the door again, shouting, and hoping someone heard her soon.

8

JAROD WALKED OUT of the police station in Walden, NY, both relieved and disappointed. Disappointed because the man they'd apprehended was not the Darren Hill they were after, but another guy with the same name. Relieved because this meant he'd be able to have more time with Lacey.

He stood silently, taking in the quiet street of the village. It was the quaint kind of upstate New York that everyone imagined on postcards. Narrow streets, trees and a picturesque white church at the center of town. Unlikely Hill would have ended up here, but every lead had to be chased down.

Jarod looked around, thinking of the small town he grew up in, and imagining he could live in a pretty town like this. Get to know his neighbors, volunteer at the school, the local fire department. His mind immediately jumped to Lacey, thinking about sharing that kind of life with her.

He shook his head, smiling to himself as he walked to the car. Lacey may have grown up on a ranch, but she was a city girl through and through. What would she do in a place like this? And why was he even thinking about it? He had no interest in leaving his home state, or his job, either.

His only interest right now, he thought with anticipation as he got into the car, was getting back to the city, and to Lacey.

LACEY STRODE out of the E.R., happy to escape. She asked the cab driver to take her directly back to the *Bliss* offices, her mind spinning. They'd insisted she be checked for smoke inhalation and other injuries even though she was fine.

The smoke had set off the sprinkler system, and she was rescued about twenty minutes after she discovered she was locked in. She'd been scared, and smelled horrible, but that was about it. She was also a wreck about her missing pictures. Intimate photos in the hands of someone who wanted to hurt her wasn't good, but who could she tell?

Only Jarod, and he wasn't here, hadn't called.

It had been complete chaos. The fire hadn't had time to do much damage, but the water had soaked things considerably, though only on the basement floor, where the damage had been contained. Still, whoever had set it meant business—the place reeked of gasoline, and if the fire had traveled much farther, catching the floor above, Lacey might not have gotten out alive.

Unfortunately, the bastard had taken all of her other work, too. The calendar shots were gone, along with everything else. How could she have slept through that? Exhausted, she knew, but still….

How could she explain this to the *Bliss* board? Her

stomach bottomed out, and she thought she'd be sick. She was due to start studio shots of Ryan Murphy, FDNY, in two hours.

Taking a deep breath, she resolved to go home, get cleaned up and deal with it when she had to. Right now, she'd save the calendar project from going up in flames, and that meant getting back here and doing what she could with Ryan today, as well as making sure she had enough pictures of Jarod.

The police were investigating motives for the fire. Coupled with what happened at her apartment and the phone calls, it was clear that someone was working out a grudge. She told them, albeit haltingly, about Scott, and they made that their first check, though she hadn't heard anything confirming or denying her ex's whereabouts.

While this was hardly her fault, she had a feeling the *Bliss* project board might not care. They were businesspeople, and if she cost them too much money, too much time, or brought in negative press, they would can her and bring in another photographer to take over. She had a meeting with them after her session with Ryan, and she needed a plan to approach them confidently, to assure them things would be fine.

If only she believed that herself.

WHEN JAROD FINALLY caught up with Lacey, he was on the edge of his patience. He'd spent his last nerve hours ago when he'd brought the car back to the police garage, and a guy he'd talked with, Lt. Ward, about Hill had told him about the *Bliss* fire.

He hadn't been able to get Lacey on the phone and something very close to fear ate at him until he spotted Jackie as he entered the *Bliss* offices.

"Is Lacey here? Is she all right?" he asked Jackie.

"She's fine. She's in a session that she rescheduled over yours."

"Where?"

Jackie shook her head. "Nope, sorry. You can't just bust in there in the middle of—"

"Jackie, I need to talk to her. Where is she?"

Jackie looked at him speculatively. "You two have quite a thing going, huh?"

Jarod wasn't going to talk about his relationship with Lacey, especially not with her assistant. "I really just want to see if she's okay. That's all. Let her know I'm back."

"She's in 3-b, the same place you had your studio— Hey!"

Jarod took off. He didn't bolt into the studio, but walked in quietly, and waited, watching Lacey, letting his eyes take in the reality that she was, in fact, all in one piece.

Why hadn't she called him? Why hadn't she let him know?

"Satisfied?" Jackie said, hands on hips.

"Not quite. When will she be done?"

"When she decides she's done," the assistant said smartly.

Jarod ignored the jibe and studied Lacey, ever the professional, taking pictures of the shirtless fireman who smiled at her as if he meant it—and Jarod found a new reason for his blood to simmer. Lacey was smiling, too, laughing and flirting, like she had done with him, and taking shot after shot.

Impatience and maybe a little bit of the green-eyed monster bit at him. He'd been worried sick, but she really was fine. He was glad for that, of course, but he wanted to touch her, and to make sure she was okay for himself. The cops said she'd gotten lucky, not to have been hurt in that fire.

When she put down the camera, whether she was done or not, he moved in, taking in her surprised expression. She was tired, too, he could see, and clearly under stress for all of her professionalism.

"Jarod—what are you doing here?"

It wasn't exactly what he expected to hear. "I've been trying to call, trying to find out if you were okay after I heard what happened. Why didn't you call me?"

She glanced from where Jackie was talking to Ryan, back to Jarod. "Why would I call you? Why didn't you call me?"

"Lacey," he started, keeping his ire in check.

"No. Don't come into my studio workplace making demands of me like you have a right to. Who do you think you are?"

Everyone had gone silent, and Jarod pulled back, wondering what was behind the defensiveness of her stance, but seeing the shadows in her eyes, he lowered his voice. "I'm the guy who's been half out of his mind hoping you were okay, that's who. I was worried sick, thinking I was gone, and someone tried to hurt you."

Harlequin Reader Service—Here's how it works: Accepting your 2 free books and 2 free mystery gifts places you under no obligation to buy anything. You may keep the books and gifts and return the shipping statement marked "cancel". If you do not cancel, about a month later we'll send you 6 additional books and bill you just $4.24 each in the U.S. or $4.71 each in Canada. That's a savings of 20% off the cover price. It's quite a bargain! Shipping and handling is just 50¢ per book.* You may cancel at any time, but if you choose to continue, every month we'll send you 6 more books, which you may either purchase at the discount price or return to us and cancel your subscription.

*Terms and prices subject to change without notice. Prices do not include applicable taxes. Sales tax applicable in N.Y. Canadian residents will be charged applicable provincial taxes and GST. Offer not valid in Quebec. All orders subject to approval. Books received may not be as shown. Credit or debit balances in a customer's account(s) may be offset by any other outstanding balance owed by or to the customer. Please allow 4 to 6 weeks for delivery. Offer available while quantities last.

NO POSTAGE
NECESSARY
IF MAILED
IN THE
UNITED STATES

BUSINESS REPLY MAIL
FIRST-CLASS MAIL   PERMIT NO. 717   BUFFALO, NY

POSTAGE WILL BE PAID BY ADDRESSEE

HARLEQUIN READER SERVICE
PO BOX 1867
BUFFALO NY 14240-9952

Send For
2 FREE BOOKS
Today!

I accept your offer!

Please send me two free *Harlequin® Blaze™* novels and two mystery gifts (gifts worth about $10). I understand that these books are completely free—even the shipping and handling will be paid—and I am under no obligation to purchase anything, ever, as explained on the back of this card.

351 HDL EYL3   151 HDL EYRR

Please Print

FIRST NAME

LAST NAME

ADDRESS

APT.#   CITY

Visit us online at
www.ReaderService.com

STATE/PROV.   ZIP/POSTAL CODE

Offer limited to one per household and not valid to current subscribers of *Harlequin® Blaze™* books.

She closed her eyes and nodded, running a hand over her face.

"Jackie, why don't you take Ryan to get a coffee and a wardrobe change, and leave us alone for a minute?"

Jackie's gaze went to Jarod, and back to Lacey. "You sure?"

"Yeah, go ahead. See you in about thirty."

"Okay," her assistant agreed and led the fireman from the studio.

"I'm sorry, Lacey. I was just imagining every awful thing when I couldn't get you on the phone. Lt. Ward told me he didn't know what happened after you went to the hospital, and the hospital wouldn't tell me anything, of course."

"I'm sorry, too. I didn't hear from you, and then there was so much to deal with, and I knew you were in the middle of your own stuff—"

"You could have called me. Should have called me," he said, pulling her in close, hugging it out, feeling the tension drain from her body as she wrapped her arms around him, too.

She shrugged. "I didn't want to bother you. I knew you were working, and I was okay."

Her pretty lips turned down as she pulled away, wrapping her arms around herself and crossing the room. When she was hurting, he realized, she pulled in, distanced herself, instead of leaning on anyone.

"Someone tried to kill you, and that's not okay. I need you to level with me, Lacey. I need to know what's going on, why someone would be doing this to you. Do you have any idea who it is? Why?"

She looked up at him, and he could see she was struggling with something, as if wondering what she should say and what she shouldn't. He didn't press anymore.

"The only person I can think of is in California, an ex of mine, and they're looking into it. I don't know who else it could be."

"Tell me about him," Jarod said gently.

She shook her head. "Not here, not now. I have to work. This is more of a mess than you know. I could lose the calendar project."

"Why? You're the victim here."

"This calendar shoot hasn't gone well from the start—people keep canceling or schedules are missing. Then there was the problem with my apartment, that cost me time, and now this fire and—" she took a deep breath, meeting his eyes "—the pictures I was developing last night were the ones of us, from the other night. But the guy took my camera bag, the digital and all of the negatives—all of them. From the shoot and from the hotel. No one knows about the, uh, personal pictures, but I'm going to have to tell *Bliss* about the rest. And why would someone take our pictures, unless they were going to try to use them somehow?"

It took a minute for her meaning to strike him. "You were developing our pictures last night?"

"Yes."

"Your ex, in California. Could he have hired someone to harass you here?"

He saw the last question had taken her by surprise, and she seemed to consider it. She faced him, a quiet determination in her eyes that made her even more beautiful to him. He wanted to touch her, protect her, and God knew what else. He wanted all of it, but there wasn't time to think about that now. Probably a good thing.

"Let me finish this session, and I'll tell you, okay? But I have to get through this, and I have to talk with the project board. There's just too much right now, Jarod."

He understood more than she realized, thinking back to the letter in the trash. He wished she could trust him more, but they'd only known each other a couple days, and he would let her have as much room as she needed.

"Sure. But I'll stay here all the same. Is there somewhere I can catch a nap? It was a long night."

She nodded. "Yes, of course, there's a break room next door. I'm sorry, I didn't ask—but since you're back, I guess you didn't get the man you're after?"

"No, we didn't. But I'm glad, or I wouldn't be here with you."

She didn't have time to answer, as Jackie and the fireman returned. Jarod watched Lacey smile, putting her professional face back on.

"I'll come get you when we're done, after my meeting, okay?"

Jarod nodded and found his way next door, though he would have rather stayed with Lacey. But soon, he planned to have his answers, and he'd make sure she was safe, one way or the other.

LACEY FACED the four-person project board hoping she appeared more confident than she was. The session with Mr. April had gone great. Ryan was an easy, fun guy who liked being photographed, but she hadn't been able to get into the groove as well as she usually did.

It was hard to look through the lens of the camera without thinking about Jarod. He was in her thoughts constantly, interfering in everything, even her work. She thought about his face, and the possessive way he'd stood there when she was working with Ryan. She didn't like jealousy, and she didn't like anything screwing with her head, but she had more pressing problems at the moment.

How did you talk to your employer about the fact that there could be compromising pictures of you floating around New York City?

She could kick herself for taking them in the first place, she thought as they all settled in, but then, as the images from the photos played in her memory, she realized she didn't regret it at all. She did, however, regret being careless and having the negatives stolen.

While honesty had always been her best policy, she decided that maybe it was best if she worked with Jarod behind the scenes to try to find out who was behind all the trouble.

However, for all she knew, it could be someone connected to one of the people in front of her—Nina, for instance, head of PR, had seemed to dislike Lacey from the start. Lacey had the distinct feeling that her hiring was not a unanimous vote.

She explained about the harassment she'd been suffering, the break-in at her apartment, and then the fire in the darkroom. Lacey didn't regret her lie of omission as much when she saw they were more concerned about their timeline and bottom line than her safety.

"If you look at the schedule, you can see we're still on the mark. We've lost some pictures, and the camera—"

"A twelve-thousand-dollar camera, Lacey," Nina said, as if Lacey had stolen it and she was too tired not to bite back.

"Yes, an expensive camera that was stolen out of a *Bliss* darkroom that I had left locked. I'm sure you have insurance to cover it," she said, and thought she saw a glint of admiration in Theo Harris's eyes. He was the head of the project board; she liked the older man who had thus far sat quietly.

"You don't need to worry about that, Lacey. We're glad you weren't hurt, but we are concerned that someone seems to be harassing you, and it could hurt the project or the magazine."

"I'm sure it won't. I won't allow that to happen, Theo. This project means everything to me, and it's really coming together well, even with the bumpy start. The police are looking into it, and I'll be careful. Please, I can finish this without any more problems. I promise. I have it under control," she assured them, meeting their eyes and hoping they bought it.

She knew she'd made the right decision not to tell them about the photos. If they found out from whoever stole them, fine—there was nothing she could do about that, but she wasn't about to dig her own grave.

"Okay, Lacey, let's table this for now. We'll see what the police say, and you keep up with the project, but I'd like daily progress reports to the board."

Lacey took a breath. "Absolutely, Theo, no problem."

She sat for a moment as the board members vacated the conference room, and thought about her close call. If she was booted from this project, word would get around, and she'd find herself taking kids' pictures with Santa. Whoever was doing this, it had to stop.

She told Jarod she'd tell him the truth. And she'd do it, too, even if it damaged what was growing between them. Lacey dropped her head into her hands, and closed her eyes, feeling trapped. Still, she didn't realize that she'd started to doze off, she was so tired.

"Hey, taking a nap?"

Lacey almost jumped out of her skin as Jackie walked into the conference room.

"You scared the life out of me," Lacey said, wiping her eyes.

"Jeez, sorry. I was just kidding," she said, "I don't care if you sneak a nap."

"Not sleeping, not really, only thinking." She noted the bandage on Jackie's hand that she must have missed earlier. "What did you do to yourself?"

Jackie smirked. "Got crazy slicing an onion the other night—five stitches, but I'm functional."

"Ouch. Onion is one mean vegetable."

Jackie grinned.

"Can I trust you with something personal?"

Jackie nodded. "Sure. Shoot."

"I need a favor."

"I'm your girl."

"Don't agree too fast and feel free to tell me to stuff it, okay?"

"Always."

"I need a list of names of people who applied for my assignment, the portfolios the board reviewed."

Jackie's eyes went wide. She obviously hadn't anticipated that. She might have thought Lacey needed something more normal, like having Jackie grab her some lunch or pick up her laundry, not corporate theft.

"I need to see the list because someone has been…giving me a hard time, and it hit me that it could be someone who wanted this job, or maybe someone who is trying to discredit me, or sabotage the project. I thought the list might be a place to start."

She told Jackie about the break-in and the pictures, and watched the shock and surprise cross Jackie's face. Lacey wrung her hands a bit, embarrassed.

"I know I shouldn't have let him take pictures like that in the first place, and I certainly shouldn't have given in to temptation and developed them here, but—"

Jackie waved her off. "Puh-lease. That's some tame stuff. Is there a couple in America that hasn't brought out the old camcorder or digital camera at least once? C'mon…this is not your fault. But I can see where you're worried. Those things could pop up anywhere, anytime, huh?"

Lacey agreed, miserable. "Pretty much. And while I might deserve to get fired, Jarod doesn't. He's really an innocent bystander in all of this."

"Not so innocent, since it was his idea to take pictures. Lucky you, I might add," said Jackie, grinning, and Lacey felt the corners of her mouth twitch.

"True, which is why I don't want him getting

screwed over by my mistake. Why I developed those here…dumb move."

"Stop beating yourself up. Let me see what I can do."

"Thanks, Jackie. I know it's asking a lot."

"Hey, I'm your go-to girl," Jackie said, though her voice sounded strained. Lacey paused on her way out of the room. "You okay?"

"Oh, yeah, I'm fine. Just a late night at the emergency room getting those stitches."

"I hear you. Take the rest of the day off. We'll start early tomorrow."

"Sure, thanks."

Lacey made her way back to her office, where Jarod had closed the window shades and was dozing on the sofa, barely big enough for him. She looked down at him sleeping, and her heart seemed to recognize his. He was gorgeous, and good through to his bones.

Still, she had to deal with the problem at hand, rather than the nasty what-ifs that were haunting her. It was why she had to tell him everything. She wanted it all to just go away, but it was never really going to, was it?

He had the resources and the know-how to track down whoever might have done this, and while it might not be Scott, it could be someone connected to him.

"Hey, Lacey."

She jumped. He was awake and looking at her.

"I thought you were still sleeping. I didn't know if I should wake you."

"C'mere," he said, holding his arms out, but she stayed back.

"I don't think it's such a good idea here."

"I'm willing to risk it," he replied with a hint of a chuckle.

She lay down over him, and admitted he was right. She needed this, too, his warmth, his strength. Everything felt better the second his arms wrapped around her. As she nestled against him she also felt a little something extra poking against her hip and wiggled appreciatively.

"There's time for that later, you vixen," he said, sounding more awake. "As tempting as you are, I haven't had a shower since yesterday, and I'm starving."

"It's three in the afternoon."

"Feels like breakfast time to me. Any place we can manage that?"

"It's New York. You can get anything any time you want it," she said.

"Sounds like my kind of place."

After some snuggling and kissing she was grateful for the reprieve as they made their way out of the building and down the street to a diner that she liked.

"So how did it go?"

"Let's eat, and I'll tell you what you want to know. We have to figure out who would be doing this, and why," she said briskly, determined to stop moping and start acting.

They sat, and as she kept herself busy for a few minutes with her flapjacks and butter, syrup and bacon, fixing her plate as he fixed his, she finally ran out of things to do and had to face the music.

"Okay. It's not a huge deal, but I do like to keep it private, especially in my work. I need to maintain a certain image…" Her voice drifted off, and she cut a bite of pancake on her plate, but then laid her fork down.

Jarod reached a long arm across the table and gently touched her hand.

"I know we haven't known each other long, and this is hard for you, but you can tell me anything, I promise. This will never go further than me."

She looked out the window at the passersby. It was getting dark earlier by small degrees, but on a cloudy day, even more so.

"Thanks. The long and the short of it is that my ex-boyfriend, Scott Myers, is the guy in California. We met when I was doing some brochure work for his company, and sort of hit it off. He was a classic California guy, looked like he spent all his time on the beach, you know?"

Jarod nodded, but added, "Eat while you talk."

Reluctantly, she picked up her fork. She was hungry and took a bite. The soothing sweetness of the comfort food helped.

"Anyway, we dated, had some fun, but a few months into it he started getting possessive, and kind of mean. It was small stuff at first, but then he actually showed up at one of my shoots and threatened a male model he thought was flirting with me. I had no idea, but he'd hired a private detective to follow me, to take pictures. I had no idea."

Jarod didn't say a word, but she noticed how his grip tightened around his fork.

"So, I told him that was it, to get lost. He claimed he was just worried about me spending all that time with male models and such, and apologized, so I thought, you know, we get along so well. I wanted to give him one more chance. It's not like I'm Miss Perfect. And up to that point, he'd never done anything to hurt me."

"But then that changed?" Jarod prompted easily when she paused, lingering over another bite.

"Yeah. It was okay for a while, seemed like it was back to how we were at first. I thought he'd just been stressed from work or whatever. But then he came home drunk as a skunk one night, and he wanted to, uh…" She stuttered, blushing and uncomfortable talking about having sex with Scott with the man she was having sex with at the moment, and Jarod seemed to get it, waving her on.

"I hear ya, and I don't need details, either."

Thank goodness.

"So I put him off. I wasn't about to deal with him in that condition. I told him to take a shower and go to bed, and when he was sober, we'd talk. The next thing I knew, I was seeing stars. It really came out of nowhere. He accused me of having sex with my models, and that's why I didn't want him. And let me assure you, though you have been an exception, you're the only one—I do not sleep with my models."

"I'm glad you made an exception, then," Jarod said, smiling, but the smile didn't reach his eyes.

"I won't detail the whole episode, but I ended up with a broken arm, and a few other cuts and bruises. It might have been worse. However I managed to get hold of a meat hammer and caught him unawares in the face. It wasn't much, but it stunned him at least. Luckily, before he came at me again, I passed out. I think maybe he thought he'd killed me because he took off. He got into a few other fights that night, he was finally arrested and tested positive for alcohol and cocaine. On combined charges, he was supposed to be away for a while, but he was recently let out on parole to home detainment for 'good behavior,'" she said with a snarl. "Good behavior, my ass."

"So that's where the scar on your arm actually came from."

"I guess I just got so used to keeping it to myself that it feels strange to talk about it. I also wanted to forget it, just let it be part of the past. No matter how I try, though, it keeps coming back up."

Jarod's expression was serious. "Did you talk to a counselor at the hospital?"

Lacey stared at her food and disentangled her fingers from his.

"I spoke to one. I went back, but it just wasn't…for me. I wanted to handle it on my own."

"I get where you're coming from."

She hadn't expected that response, and her surprise showed.

"You do?"

"Sure. I've been forced into my share of shrink appointments—it's SOP after certain things, like the first time I had to shoot someone and they died in front of me. The first time I lost a friend, a fellow Ranger—that one was harder. Sometimes it helps, sometimes it doesn't. What I do know is you have to be open to it for it to do any good, and no one can force you into it. If you're not ready, you're not ready."

Relief thrummed through her. "So you just dealt with it on your own?"

"For a while. I was able to handle the fact that I'd had to use my gun. I grew up in a house with a Ranger, and I knew that carrying that weapon meant probably having to use it. But, when my friend Matt was killed, that was tough. I thought I could shake it, but I couldn't."

"How did he die?"

"We were having a beer after a bad day—you know, winding down? We'd just caught a guy who'd been causing some pretty serious trouble around town for a while."

Jarod picked up a piece of bacon then put it down again. Her heart hurt at his carefully controlled expression, the way he didn't let much show, when there was so much going on inside.

"Turns out his younger brother was his partner in crime, not that the kid had much choice. He was barely out of his teens. We didn't even know about him. As we left the bar, the kid walked up to us and shot Matt. There was no talk, no warning, nothing. Just a gunshot, point-blank in the chest. Matt was dead before he hit the ground."

"Oh, my God," Lacey breathed, horrified. "And then?"

"The kid was dead a second later."

Lacey stared, unable to get her mind around what he was saying. How was it possible he dealt with ordeals like that on a regular basis?

"I—I don't know what to say, Jarod. It's unthinkable." She stood, crossed to him and slid into the booth on his side and wrapped her arms around his shoulders. "How do you deal with that? How can anyone deal with that?"

"That's kind of the point," he said calmly, taking her hands and kissing them. "I couldn't. I had gone through the motions with the shrink before, and made out okay. I thought I could handle this, too, and I crashed, big-time. Got in a tight spot a few weeks later and almost shot an innocent person, and that's when I knew something was fried in my brain from what had happened with Matt. So I went for counseling. It took a while, but I made peace with it."

"How?"

"Talking it through, reliving it, saying what I had to say—realizing there wasn't anything I could have done to stop it."

Lacey felt tears prick her eyelids. She couldn't say anything. She felt like a coward, whining about her onetime altercation with Scott when others went through so much worse. She said as much, and Jarod dislodged her hold, pulled away.

"Lacey, that's not why I told you that story, because it's not something I share often, either, and it wasn't meant to make what happened to you smaller."

"But it seems so—"

"No. What I'm trying to say is that if you can't quite get away from this, it's because you haven't let it go.

You won't be able to let it go until you figure out a way to work through it."

She went back to her seat. "You do think I should see a counselor."

"I didn't say that. I don't know what's right for you. You need to figure it out. You were attacked, but you also fought back. You hit him and you kept yourself from likely being killed. That's huge. You're a fighter. Don't let him win now by letting it eat you up inside. By being afraid all the time."

Lacey listened, took in what he was saying, though she didn't know what to do. She didn't know if counseling was the answer. But what he said about letting it go made sense. Still…how?

"You've helped," she said in a whisper, her gaze meeting his. "I knew, somehow, when I saw you with that little girl—maybe before that—that you were the complete opposite of him. That I could…be with you."

"I'm glad about that," he said, smiling, and this time the smile did fill his eyes.

She took a deep breath. "I suppose it felt good to finally tell someone, too—you—and to hear your story. Everyone has their stories, I guess."

"Yes. But that doesn't make yours any less important."

"Maybe." She picked up a bite of pancake and though it was now just lukewarm, it tasted much better than before, when she hadn't been able to taste anything. She caught the spark of heat in Jarod's gaze as he followed her progress, watching her slip the morsel between her lips. She warmed inside, but with more than desire.

He still wanted her. He didn't see her as weak, or less sexy, or as a victim. Nothing she told him had turned him off. In fact, she was pretty sure from the light in his eyes that he was very much the opposite of turned off. She looked at the syrup on the table, and said, "You know, I wonder if they do takeout?"

He groaned and shook his head, smiling.

Later. Definitely later. She planned to lick him clean.

"I know it's not Scott," she said, switching gears and returning to their original problem. "I called Legal Aid today and spoke to their assistant, Gena, who said he's still in California under house arrest."

"That makes it harder to figure out who it could be, but we'll find him."

"I asked Jackie to get me the list of people who were in line for this project. Maybe I'll recognize a name, or we might find someone who wanted to sabotage the project, or something."

"That's smart."

She smiled, the praise igniting a warm glow inside. "Thanks for listening, Jarod, and thanks for not seeing me as a victim."

"Are you kidding me? With your spirit? No way. You're one of the strongest women I've ever met, and one of the most gorgeous."

"You're not so bad yourself."

"Oh, honey, I have yet to show you just how bad I can be," he said smoothly, a wicked promise in his eyes.

She hoped he planned to, and bought the extra bottle of syrup, just in case.

9

THE NEXT DAY, atop the Empire State Building, the second shoot wasn't going as well as the Central Park work. The problems of the past few days were taking their toll. Jarod wanted to help, but he wasn't sure how. Lacey had done okay with Ryan, who went before him so that he could still make his shift at the firehouse on time, but now she seemed to be having a hard time. Jarod wondered if it was him, or the cumulative stress.

He tried distracting himself by watching the amazing vista of the city laid out below him, but his mind would only travel back to Lacey.

She'd already broken one lens. Her clumsy fingers were probably caused by lack of sleep and nerves, and she was cursing as she couldn't get the shots she wanted just the way she wanted them. Which meant he was bent and folded into yet more ridiculous poses and fluffed and primped even more. It grated on his own bad mood, but he put up with it because it was Lacey, and she didn't need him complaining.

"Shit, shit, shit!" she shouted in frustration, and put the camera down, he figured, so that she didn't end up throwing it.

He pushed past the stylist and crossed the platform, took her by the arm and led her into the lobby through the doors where they could be alone for a few minutes. He saw her cast a concerned glance back at the crew, who watched them curiously as they disappeared from view, but he didn't give a rat's ass what anyone else thought at the moment.

"Hey, come here," he said, pulling her in and rubbing his hands over the stress-hardened muscles of her back until he felt her relax and soften against him. "Not such a good day, huh?"

"Work usually distracts me from anything bothering me, but today, I just can't seem to clinch it. Everything is swirling in my head and I can't focus," she said, banging her forehead softly against his chest. "I felt like I rushed Ryan through, and I can't get these shots right, either, and I have to get a progress report in by four," she said in exasperation.

The scent of her shampoo wafted up, and he found himself thinking about more erotic things than comforting her. He'd love to get back in the shower with her, work soap through those short, silky locks and move his hands down the length of her body, touching every inch of water-slick skin. He'd make sure she was relaxed.

"Let's see if I can't settle down some of the things spinning around in there," he said seductively, leaning down to capture her mouth in a soft kiss. She stiffened in surprise at first, probably worried about someone seeing them, but only for a second before a wildfire erupted between them. All of the emotions they both had bottled up channeled through the kiss until his hands were inside her shirt, thumbs caressing her nipples into tight peaks. In return she was slowly rocking her pelvis into his erection.

Another minute of this and he was going to haul her up and have her on the spot; instead, he lowered his hands and exerted some self-control. Truth be told, he'd needed to touch her pretty badly, and the short tryst had helped his own mood considerably. Just being near her seemed to help, soothing his worries and frustrations. He couldn't remember any other woman having that effect on him before. He wasn't sure he was the same guy who'd landed in the city just a few days ago, when his job had been the center of his universe.

"Still thinking too much?" he asked against the delicate shell of her ear, planting a kiss there and enjoying her gasp of a response. Encouraged, he slipped his fingers under the top of her pants and caressed the soft, secret spots just below the small of her back.

"Only about getting you out of your pants," she said baldly, her breath quickening at his touch, and he laughed.

"Hold on to that thought. Any chance we can hang back here for a bit when they leave?"

She looked at him in surprise, and he loved how her eyes sparked with pleasure and adventure as she realized what he was asking. Whatever had happened to her in the past with the bastard who had broken her arm, she hadn't lost who she was. Jarod was just glad that he got to be the man who helped her learn that, as well.

"I think we might be able to arrange that. Not for

long, their security is pretty strict, but I bet I could wrangle enough time for…a quickie."

"Sounds fun. Something to look forward to. Let's get back out there and finish this, then, huh?"

She smiled at him, nodding, and his heart did an untrustworthy flip that he purposely ignored.

Feeling considerably better, they both went back out to the deck, noticing the crew's determination not to make eye contact. Jarod took his position against the rails again, and watched as she lost the stiffness that had held her before. Her moves were more fluid now as she captured him through the camera.

When she aimed the camera at him, it was like a touch. The memory of her taste came back to him, her scent. He thought about her face when he was inside of her, how her irises darkened. Sometimes her lashes fell down as she came, her mouth forming a soundless O, and other times she looked straight through him, letting him see and hear every nuance of the pleasure he gave her. Thinking about Lacey's expressions during orgasm, he could barely hold back his body's response.

He followed her instructions, happy to do whatever pleased her. After a while he started to focus on the way her skin took on a fine sheen of perspiration from the physicality of her work with the camera. She squatted down and leaned in, the scoop of her low-cut tee revealing tender flesh. His fingers flexed, wanting to rediscover the velvety texture of her nipples. How much longer did they have to do this? How many pictures could she possibly need?

When he heard the slight hum of the zoom, he concentrated, hoping she could read everything he wanted to do to her in his eyes. And that he didn't think he could wait much longer. Thankfully the pants he was wearing were baggy, because he had a boner that would challenge the tower rising above them. He smiled in satisfaction when he saw her pink lips part below the camera's edge. She was as turned on as he was.

They were both on edge by the time she called it quits—two wardrobe changes and about a million pictures later. No one would be able to tell except for him. She went through all the professional motions, wrapping it up, excusing the crew, telling security they were staying to do some extra shots.

Jarod didn't waste time when he saw the security team accompany the crew to the elevator, leaving them alone until a guard came back to escort them out.

"We have about ten minutes, give or take, by the time he gets back up here," she said, taking Jarod by the hand and pulling him over to one side of the observation deck overlooking the Chrysler Building.

"No problem. I want you so much I've been ready to come for the past twenty minutes."

He had her low rise capris unbuttoned and unzipped before she could answer, his fingers dipping under the delicate material of her thong and in between soft folds of flesh. She was already wet, hot and ready for him. He'd never been so thankful in his life.

"Jarod," she panted, and he thought maybe she was going to protest, but she just broke their kiss to say, "Get these off." She pulled at his jeans, releasing his cock with nimble hands.

"Good thinking," he said, turning her so that they were both propped against the ledge, looking down over the city. He slid inside from behind in a hot thrust that had him closing his eyes to the amazing view.

She gasped, moving back against him, and he lifted her tee, closing his hands over her breasts. He could barely wait to explode inside of her.

"That photo session was so hot…the way you were looking at me," she said, her tone husky and trembling with desire, "I couldn't wait for them to leave so I could fuck you."

He loved how she talked dirty, and he found his desire pushed up a few more notches, if that were possible.

"Good. Tell me more, what you want, just like that," he said, wanting to hear her demands, her needs, and wanting to meet every single one of them.

She would always surprise him, and he welcomed it.

"You want to hear how I love feeling you get harder when you're inside me? How it was all I thought about while I was taking those pictures?"

"Yes," he said roughly, increasing his pace. "I wondered if you were getting wet as you were looking at me through the lens, and I remembered how you taste, how hot, sweet…"

She groaned and moved her hips in rhythm with his thrusts. It was heaven.

Until he realized they didn't have protection and his mind screamed in protest. How could he have forgotten?

"*Lacey,*" he panted, fighting for control at the way she was writhing against him. "I'm not wearing anything," he said, although the heated silky flesh of her sex felt tight around his shaft and he didn't want to leave. But he would if he had to, even if it killed him.

She paused slightly, and surprised him again. "It's okay, we're good, I'm on the pill, I just wanted to be extra careful before...just don't stop, please," she begged in the sweetest way possible, pushing her hips up and rotating her ass in a way that made him tremble.

LACEY WAS MORE THAN HAPPY to forget everything in the world except the wonderful, wet, gliding sensation of Jarod's cock as she looked out over the dizzying view.

Power rippled through her, emotional freedom mixing with physical pleasure. He'd set loose her true nature. This was *her.* She was wild, willing to do anything he wanted, anywhere, and she reveled in the feeling. Staring at the sky and the expanse of the world below, she knew she'd never felt more free in her life.

His eyes had telegraphed one sexual promise after another as she'd snapped the pictures, and nearly had her coming before they'd even finished the session. She was halfway there before he even touched her, and it pleased her that she could tell him what she wanted, how she wanted it, and her lack of inhibition only seemed to drive him further.

They didn't have time for inhibition—the guard could be back any moment, catching them, and the idea just made her hotter, made her want it more. When she imagined what someone would see, how they looked going at it here in the open, a low moan worked its way up from her chest, the arousal almost too much.

He held her tight around the waist, and she savored every second of it as the sizzling sensation set off a myriad of others. Her inner muscles then gripped him in spasms of pleasure against his thrusts until he was so deep she was sure he was touching her soul. She'd never cared for being done from the back, the facelessness of it bothered her, but with Jarod, she was fully aware of whom she was with, and only wanted more.

His body took its cue from hers, the heat of his own orgasm throbbing and flooding inside of her. He bucked hard, his hands grasping the soft skin of her bottom as he pushed harder, deeper, which sent another spike of release rocketing through her.

Finally, they stilled, but the pleasure was so complete and so lingering she didn't want to let go. The residual sensations traveled everywhere in her body, even to the ends of her fingers and toes. She didn't want to return to the real world, to thinking.

She wanted to stay up here with him and keep feeling this way… or stay anywhere with him and keep feeling this way? *Maybe,* she thought fuzzily.

"Mmm…" She turned and nuzzled his mouth with her lips, sharing lazy, satisfied kisses. If she waited a little, she knew the embers settling between them would spark again.

Until they heard the buzz—the elevator was back.

"Oh, no," they said in unison, laughing and pushing

apart, shuffling to a far spot where they quickly got their clothes in order.

Lacey grabbed her camera in a desperate attempt to look as if they were finishing up a few pictures, but instead, she collapsed, chuckling at the fun of it. Her heart hammered at almost being caught, literally, with her pants down. She could only grin at Jarod as the guard appeared, looking bored and stoic.

She took a few shots, and for fun, grabbed a couple of the surprised guard, as well, before they headed back down to the ground and back to reality.

10

"I SHOULD HAVE GONE back to the labs. You know, to make up for the time I lost," Lacey said, staring at the ceiling and catching her breath after another bout of amazing sex with Jarod. She rolled over, covering him with her body, loving how big and warm he was. She threaded her fingers through his chest hair, leaning in to nibble a flat, brown male nipple until he moaned for mercy.

"There's always time for work."

"Maybe. I feel like I need to do double time these days, to make up for all the problems."

"Has anyone said anything else?"

"No. I just e-mail in a progress report, and everything seems okay. There hasn't been anything said about the pictures. Maybe you're right, and whoever took them had no idea, or didn't think they were worthwhile, or whatever. I have no idea."

The reminder was a splash of cold water. She really should have gone back to work, but the lovemaking up on the Empire State Building had been so exhilarating they'd been unable to take their hands off each other after, and had barely made it back to her apartment for more.

Lacey had had several lovers in her life—nice guys, great guys and some obviously lackluster ones, too— but she'd never been as voraciously hungry for anyone as she was for Jarod. Just looking at him lounging in her bed was enough to make her throw all of her priorities out the window and…what?

They hadn't talked about anything. They didn't have any kind of relationship or plans or promises. All they had was this, what they were doing right now.

"Hey…you're clouding up. What's wrong?"

"Oh, I'm sorry. I guess it's just back to reality with a thud. I really should have worked—tomorrow is Saturday, and maybe I can make up some time this weekend, because Monday will be the last shoot we'll be doing…"

She let the thought drift, and felt a slight pang when he didn't fill the void. So that was that, apparently. Come Monday, this little fling would be done.

What had she expected?

"Listen, Lacey, there's something you need to know, and I guess I should have told you before now, but…well, I guess I was pretty happy being distracted from reality, too."

Lacey took a deep breath. *Here it comes,* she thought. His gentle letdown, the reminder that they never had more than sex, the long goodbye.

"There's an APB out on Scott. Apparently he found a way to hack the ankle alarm so that it didn't go off, or he paid someone who knew how to do it. It's been reading as if he's there in the house. No one checked until he didn't show up for work. He could have gone anytime the night before, so he has a good lead."

Lacey was stunned. That wasn't what she'd expected at all.

"When did you find out?" she asked in a whisper. "How can that be? I called…"

"You called your Legal Aid office, and you spoke to the assistant Gena, right?" he asked gently, reaching for her hand and squeezing.

"Yes."

"She's missing now, too. They think she's been working with him, using her position to help him out. She was probably covering for him when you called."

"Gena? She's involved with Scott?" It was too bizarre.

"Apparently they got together during your case, and kept it under wraps, but they found letters from her in his house, indicating an affair."

Lacey processed what he was telling her, and as the picture clarified, so did her anger. "She knew where I was, and she told him. He was probably using her to find me, knowing him. He's not stupid."

"Possibly, which means she'd be in danger now, too."

She shook her head. The whole thing was surreal. Gena had always been such a doll to her, so sincere and convincing. But then, Scott could put on a good act, too. *Poor Gena,* Lacey thought, feeling sorry for the woman, and fearful for what could have happened to her.

"Why didn't you tell me right away?" she asked, unable to keep the accusation from her voice.

"At first, I didn't want to disturb your work. You

were having such a hard time. And I figured, as long as you were with me, you're safe. I wouldn't let him get within ten feet of you, you know that," Jarod said seriously, sitting up and edging close.

"So he's here," she said flatly. "Fine. Let him find me. Then it will be settled."

"Yes, it will be because I'm not leaving your side until it is."

"Jarod, we'll be done with work on Monday, and you have to go back, and—"

"I have vacation time coming, and I'm not going back until I know you're safe—already told you that. Unless…you'd like me to leave?"

She wouldn't have believed it if she hadn't seen it herself, the speck of uncertainty that flickered in his gorgeous eyes as he asked the question. And leaned down to kiss her fingers where their hands were folded together. She shook her head.

"No, I don't want you to go. That's kind of a problem, too, don't you think?"

"I don't know. It's certainly not something I counted on, getting in this deep this fast, but I can't say I regret it," he said, sliding a hand under her chin and leaning in for a kiss.

"Me, either," she admitted, noting how the heated desire that was automatic between them was picking up a warmth that it lacked before. A deeper sense of connection as they admitted, just a little, that what they had might be more than a fling.

"Good. We'll do this together. You're not alone," he promised, drawing her against him so tenderly that her eyes pricked with tears, but she blinked them back. This was good. Jarod was good, and things were going to be okay. She had to believe that.

She ran a hand along the inside of his thigh, marveling at his strength, inside and out.

"If he's watching, then the best thing to do, the fastest way to end this, is to take control of the game. It's the weekend. Let's go out. We'll be tourists, we'll be visible, we'll make it clear we're lovers, which won't be an effort at all," Jarod murmured against her skin.

"You want to flush him out?" she asked, shivering, but not from fear. The idea of taking control, of ending this on her terms—their terms—was appealing.

He kissed her shoulder, tasting her lightly with his tongue all the way down to her elbow.

Her professional life was at risk, and her crazy ex was on the loose, and yes, all she could do was admire how gorgeous Jarod's body was. The mutual agreement that they had something special between them, regardless of where it was leading, was a definite turn-on. She shifted a little, letting her hand move higher on his thigh, her palm closing over his cock, stroking him to hardness.

Nestled in his lap, his hand wound in her hair, the sheets tangled warmly around them, she sighed against his skin, knowing a moment of perfect connection and happiness unlike any she had known before. Right now, here with him, she didn't want to think about anything but Jarod. The rest would come soon enough.

He smelled great, musky and male. Their scents mingled, seducing her, and she shifted a little more until she could rub her lips over the head of his erection in a way she knew he liked. She smiled at the murmur of approval, the shudder that worked its way down his long body.

Using her hands and her mouth, she wanted to bring him more pleasure than he could imagine. She set about the task with steady purpose, inventive in her kisses as she kept him in her throat, curling her soft tongue along his length like a lazy cat. She continued teasing the tender skin of his sex until he was gasping mindless exclamations, his body hard and rigid, held taut under her own.

Her fingers gently stroked his legs, stomach and sac, keeping him on edge. When she sensed he was about to come, she pressed firmly on the area below his scrotum while sucking him to orgasm once, and holding back his ejaculation successfully.

He pushed up on his elbows, panting, as she slid her mouth down over him again and erotically met his gaze.

"How…?"

She released him from her sexy kiss and smiled. "Little tantric secret I learned…it makes it so you can come more than once, and it's more intense. Was it?"

"My head nearly came off my shoulders," he confessed, shaking his head in amazement.

"How about we try it again?"

"Sure. You can join me this time," he said with a sexy growl. Suddenly, he rolled her over into the mattress, his knee pushing her thighs apart as he pulled her calves over his shoulders and his cock found the slick entrance to her body.

"You're close, too," he said, sliding a finger down between her legs and she couldn't help but cry out.

"Sucking you makes me hot," she admitted plainly, and was rewarded as he took her mouth in a deep kiss, fucking her mouth with his tongue as he thrust into her body, both of them starving in spite of all the previous loving.

He moved her legs down off his shoulders, staying inside her, but he gentled and slowed his strokes, making her wait, making them both wait as he framed her face with his hands.

"I can't seem to get enough of you…"

"I feel the same way," she said, even though her heart was crying out words that were too soon to say—right?

All words quickly became unimportant as they held on for as long as they could. They moved more quickly, then slowed—a few times stopping altogether to see how long they could take it. He also showed her a few of his own tricks to prolong their anticipation and their pleasure. Finally, need took over and drove them both to release; hands clasped, they were connecting even more deeply than perhaps they knew, or were ready for.

Jarod collapsed over her, and then moved to cuddle her into his side.

Lacey was limp from satisfaction, and maybe a little sore, but that even felt okay. Dozing, it took her a minute to realize the sound she heard in the background was the ringing of her phone.

Pushing herself up, she grabbed her cell from the table with a sense of trepidation, but saw Jackie's name show on the screen and felt relief instead. "It's just Jackie."

At the same time, Jarod's phone rang; and they smirked, their peaceful moment well and truly intruded upon.

"It's Tom, my captain—it's still afternoon there, work hours—I have to take this."

"No problem, I need to call Jackie back, too. She was getting the list of other applicants for us, but I don't know if we'll need it."

"Get it anyway. Can't hurt to cover all the bases."

"Sure," she said with a sigh, hoping that no matter what, this would all be over soon.

"Jackie? Hi, yeah, Lacey. If you're calling about the list—what? Oh, no…"

Jackie was calling from the hospital. Someone had attacked her, and Lacey had a terrible feeling that Scott had found yet another victim.

JAROD PINCHED the bridge of his nose between his thumb and forefinger, staving off a headache. He had to get off the phone and go with Lacey to the hospital, but he'd gotten a dose of his own bad news. Although it wasn't as bad as it could have been.

"Tom, any chance we can dust that envelope for prints?" Jarod asked.

"Already sent it—left the pictures in my desk drawer, of course."

"Dammit all to hell. I understand if you have to report—"

He didn't get any further.

"Jarod, there's no way I'd tell anyone about this, and with any luck, we can clean it up quietly. You think this is the same guy who's stalking the, uh, woman in the photos? And I'm sorry that I looked at them, it just took me a few minutes to process what it was I was looking at, until the note dropped out. Seems like someone is taking a serious shot at your reputation, and there's no way I'm letting that happen to any of my officers, least of all you."

"Well, we think we know who's behind it. A man named Scott Myers. He was Lacey's boyfriend, broke her arm, hurt her some before he got sent away."

"Son of a bitch."

"Yeah. She's the photographer on the shoot, so this could cost her her job, as well. I want this guy as soon as possible so we're going to try to flush him out."

"You watch your step, Jarod, and maybe bring the local guys in on this, especially if you're involved with this woman."

Jarod took a deep breath, knowing Tom was right. "I'll contact a guy."

"Is this thing serious?"

"Hell, yeah, this guy is—"

"Not the case, the girl," Tom said, laughing.

Jarod paused, feeling foolish. He looked up when he heard the shower turn on. "Yes, I think it's getting there."

"Then taking this promotion might be good for you—keep you alive longer, home more—unless you're thinking of moving to New York?"

"No, no, nothing like that."

"So you want the job? I have to know if you're going for it."

"What about the pictures?"

"What about them? Some asshole is trying to ruin your reputation, and I'm not letting that get in the way of my best man moving up. You didn't do anything illegal there, well, maybe in Texas, but as you're in New York…" Tom teased, and Jarod found himself grinning. Some of the stuff he'd done with Lacey, and what he wanted to do, was probably illegal in several states.

"Thanks, Tom. But, yeah, put my name in and I'll go through the paperwork when I get back this week."

"Good news, Jarod. I was worried there for a bit."

"I have to go, Tom. Later," Jarod said, hanging up.

He couldn't think about this now. Lacey had mentioned something about her assistant, Jackie, being hurt, and he needed to get cleaned up to go with Lacey to the hospital. He knew she feared it was her ex, but why go after the assistant?

Pulling the shower door aside, he let his eyes wander over her supple, soapy form. He joined her under the spray and couldn't imagine not seeing Lacey like this, in his shower, in his bed, in his life, every day.

But that was a long leap from where they were now, and he wasn't sure how they'd get it to work. First things first, he thought, planting a light kiss on her lips, and hoping that soon all they had to worry about was how they'd manage to be together.

LACEY'S HANDS SHOOK as she walked down the hospital hallway, searching for Jackie's room, so she stuffed them in the pockets of her pants. She didn't want Jarod to see how freaked out she was.

When they'd been making love and talking about how they could pull Scott out of hiding, she'd felt all fired up by adrenaline and desire. However, as she turned the corner and saw her friend's bruised face, she had to maintain her composure—for Jackie's sake—but was reminded of how dangerous Scott was. This was no game.

Lacey walked to Jackie's bedside, taking her hand gently.

"Oh, Jackie, I am so sorry. Who did this?"

Jackie shook her head. "I don't know. Some guy. He jumped me on the way out of the office, by the alley on Third. I thought he was a mugger, but he grabbed me and asked me where you were."

"Where I was? But how could he expect you to know?"

"I didn't know…I h-had no idea," Jackie said, tears filling her eyes.

"Shh. You don't have to talk about it."

"No, it's okay. Thank God someone saw him, called for help, and when I looked later, I saw that the list was gone. He took everything in my bag, including the list."

"The list?"

"With the names of the other people who had applied for the calendar project. He took that, though who knows why…"

Jarod spoke softly. "He probably figured you had contact information in there somewhere. I'll talk to the NYPD, explain, and see if they can get someone on your door in case he comes back."

Jackie's eyes opened wide in fear. Lacey shot Jarod

a look, but she knew he was right. Abusive men were often so determined to find their exes that they didn't even care what happened to themselves, or to others, as long as they achieved some kind of vengeance for being denied.

Which meant she was going to do just as Jarod said, and make it easy for the bastard—he'd gone too far this time, and she wasn't going to let anyone else she cared about be hurt.

She squeezed Jackie's hand as Jarod went outside to make his call.

"Don't worry. This will be over soon."

Jackie tried to smile with a cut lip. "I know. You two… He's pretty amazing, huh?"

Lacey felt her cheeks warm, and couldn't resist a smile. "Yeah, he really is."

"I'm glad. You deserve it after what you've been through."

Lacey stilled. "What do you mean?"

Jackie paused at her tone, shrugging. "Just that with all the harassment, your apartment, the horrible thing on your wall, the pictures being stolen… It's good that there's something positive coming out of this for you."

Lacey relaxed.

"Thanks. I'm just so sorry this happened to you."

"Hey, a few days of rest and watching TV. It'll be fine, until the painkillers wear off. This is some great stuff," Jackie joked bravely, and Lacey forced herself to laugh, though she felt like doing quite the opposite.

"Where's Kenny?"

"He was here earlier, but he had to work."

Jarod appeared in the doorway, and Jackie's eyes fluttered shut. Lacey squeezed Jackie's hand again. "I'm going to go now, but you don't worry—and get some rest. I'll be back. Call me if you need anything, or just to talk."

"Thanks," Jackie murmured sleepily, dozing off before Lacey reached the door.

She looked Jarod in the eye. "This has to end."

"It will. They're going to notify hospital security and get the floor guard to make more stops. It's the best they can do. They can't post a cop up here if they aren't even sure it was Scott."

"I'm sure," Lacey said resolutely.

"Jackie didn't have a good description. It could have been anyone."

"Of course it wasn't just anyone—who would attack my assistant and take her work bag? He didn't even take her money!"

"The police can't spare the resources unless they have more compelling evidence, is all. It's the way of things," Jarod explained, steering her down the hall.

"So what do we do now?"

"We get some food, get some sleep, and tomorrow, we play tourist until we flush out the creep. With the APB it won't be easy for him to walk around. He's a wanted man."

Lacey nodded. Walking out into the humid night, she tried to feel better, but as they headed down the dark street, she wondered if they were being watched.

In case they were, she stopped and pushed up on tiptoes, wrapping her arms around Jarod's neck. She then delivered a kiss that was worthy of stopping in the middle of a busy New York thoroughfare.

"Wow. What was that for?" Jarod asked as she drew away.

"Just because," she answered lightly, planting another quick kiss before falling back into step at his side, hoping Scott was watching and that he got the point.

11

"RELAX, LACEY. You're strung as tight as a bow wire," Jarod said, slinging an arm around her shoulders to pull her close and plant a kiss atop her head.

"I know. It's just so weird to be walking out here, pretending to have a good time, enjoying a Saturday stroll in the park. As bait."

"You're not bait. Not really. You're really the hunter, remember. We're in control because he doesn't know we're setting a trap. Besides, I'm here, and everything will be fine, okay?"

He reassured her while his eyes covertly scanned the scene around them. He wanted to make sure of two things: that Scott Myers had ample opportunity to see them, and that they passed by enough less-populated parts of the park that if the guy decided to make his move, he'd do it, thinking Jarod was completely distracted and unaware.

Surprise.

His forty-five was snug against his hip on the opposite side of where Lacey snuggled in, and Jarod wouldn't hesitate to use it, if that's what it came to. Her safety was first. Jarod would make sure that Scott never bothered her again, one way or the other.

"Do you like museums?" she asked.

"Some."

"There's the Met ahead of us, which is awesome, and the natural history museum is farther up. There's also the zoo, and the Conservatory Garden…"

"This park is so vast. I never really had a chance to appreciate it until now," he observed, getting into the spirit. Children played, running down slopes of shallow rises. In another spot, a small dog chased a ball, running happily back to its owner. Lovers found a more private spot, setting up camp for the day under a large tree, the city towering in the backdrop. People carried coffees and books, looking for a place to lounge, and runners and bikers came into view as if appearing from thin air.

Saturday morning in the park was an event all its own.

"I wasn't here to sightsee the last time I was here, of course."

"That must have been horrible. I saw it on the news. I was in California then, but I have a new understanding of it, being here, even now."

"Yeah, it was…overwhelming."

She looked up at him, her beautiful eyes hidden behind enormous, purple-shaded sunglasses.

"I can't imagine you being overwhelmed by anything."

He pondered telling her just how much she pulled the rug right out from under him every time she looked his way, but shrugged instead.

"I don't think anyone walked away from that situation the same person they were when they walked into it." He found he really didn't want to talk about it, not here in the sunshine and on such a beautiful day. "But no more of that. I vote for the zoo. I haven't been to a zoo since I was a kid."

"Really? I usually make it a point to visit them whatever city I'm in."

"I always felt sorry for the animals, cooped up instead of out, roaming freely."

"Where poachers and lack of habitat threaten them daily?"

"True. The world's not the same for anyone anymore, is it? Not even the lions, tigers and bears."

"No, but the world's also filled with people who protect all of us—like you, for instance."

He didn't have anything to say in response to the blatant admiration in her voice, and it touched something deep inside of him when she held on to his arm more tightly and pressed her cheek against him.

"I guess it's a little bent to say I'm enjoying myself, even considering the circumstances," she said with a rueful laugh as they made their way to the zoo. "Pretty sad when even luring out a felon is a way for us to spend time together," she joked, but didn't really think it was funny.

"No way, I'm enjoying this, too. In fact," he said playfully, pulling her over against a huge boulder to their left, "let me show you how much."

He removed her sunglasses and shoved them in his pocket, pushing hair back from her face. He looked at her closely, noticing faded freckles across her cheeks, adding interest to porcelain skin. She had some bright flecks in the green of her eyes, and as he studied her, he smiled as pink tinted her cheeks.

He took his time, able to see their surroundings, so he could take a moment to commit every feature to his memory.

Mindful of a nearby family, he leaned in, bracing his hands on the rock behind Lacey, pressing soft kisses all over her face until she was laughing, but also breathing a little more quickly. He found her mouth and slid his tongue lightly over her upper and bottom lip, no other parts of their bodies touching at all, though they were begging to.

"It would take forever for me to kiss you in all the ways I think about doing," he said, balancing his forehead against hers. "You know this isn't the end of this, right?"

She cupped her small hand around his face in a gesture so sweet that he was embarrassed to admit he turned to mush.

"I'd like that, but you know, maybe it's just the circumstances, the urgency of it all. I don't expect any promises, Jarod," she said, but he held his hand up to stop her.

"I've had my share of one-night stands, and in fact it's all I've known, more or less. I figured that's what we were doing, too, but I know better now. I want more. I don't know how, but we'll work it out, won't we?"

Her face became radiant in the sunlight, and while he knew marriage to a cop was a stupid bet—thinking about his parents' relationship disintegrating—there was no way he could live without Lacey. He'd go for the captain's position, and get it. It would give him a more normal schedule, and he could find more weekends, vacation time, to make it to New York, if that's what it took.

"I'm just so glad none of this touched you."

"You've touched me," he said, feeling silly, but it was true. There was no way he was telling her about the pictures reaching Tom—with any luck, that wouldn't amount to anything. Except some embarrassment that his friend and his boss had seen some pretty intimate moments in his life.

The thought reminded him of why they were there, and he pushed back from the rock, handing her glasses to her.

"To the zoo?"

She smiled, full on, and Jarod realized he was going to have to get used to a whole new set of emotions being around this woman.

"Lead the way," he said, grabbing her hand as he did a quick check of their surroundings. Nothing.

Could they be completely off base? He reminded himself to be patient. It was still early. Maybe their stalker was off to a slow start.

LACEY COULDN'T BELIEVE what a fantastic time she was having. She felt on top of the world as they made their way slowly through the zoo, watching the animals, sneaking into secret places to steal kisses and sometimes a little bit more.

This was real, she thought. It had come out of nowhere when she'd least expected it, but what she felt for Jarod was growing in leaps and bounds every second, and it was real.

So what did that mean? Did she give up everything she'd worked for and move to a small town in Texas to be a wife and mother?

No. That wasn't her style.

Did he come to New York? He hadn't mentioned anything specific, just that he didn't want what they had to end. But she had a feeling Texas was a part of him, just like his job.

So, a long-term, long-distance relationship?

She had friends who made it work, in fact, who flourished in those situations, but she'd never considered it for herself. She wanted the whole enchilada, her career, and the man in her life to be around to cuddle up with at night, to discuss the events of the day, and not on the phone.

But she also wanted Jarod and she supposed she'd do what she must to have him.

In spite of the complications, she felt ridiculously light. It was midafternoon, and they strolled slowly from the zoo, taking the long way, stopping to sit in the stretch of shadows created by trees as the sun passed overhead. Casually touching, they were always making some contact.

It was good.

She had almost completely forgotten about why they'd come there in the first place, and it seemed that maybe they'd made a mistake. Scott wasn't stupid, and perhaps he wasn't going to be lured out while she was with Jarod—he'd wait until she was alone. She shared as much with Jarod as they walked.

"If you're saying I should leave you alone to deal with him, forget it," Jarod said resolutely, his expression hardening.

It tweaked her a little. She appreciated his protection, and she certainly didn't want to take on Scott by herself, but she was still an independent person, making her own decisions.

"I'm just saying, you have to go back to Texas this week, and he's probably waiting for that."

"He doesn't have the time—he's an escaped felon, and all of those circumstances are going to push him to act fast, and make a mistake. Trust me, I've been here a million times."

"I know, but I know Scott. He's not stupid."

Picking up on her tone, he nodded. "So what are you saying?"

"Maybe we could part ways? I'll walk home on my own, you could go to pick up some food or something? I'll stay out in the open, among people, so I'll be safe, and I have my phone. We can see if he shows then."

"I don't like it. It makes you too vulnerable. He's desperate, and desperate men do crazy things."

"Jarod, I'd be perfectly safe on midtown streets, and maybe you could follow behind, then, or we could have a signal."

"A signal?"

The way that he asked that made her feel as if he wasn't taking her seriously. She didn't like it and said as much.

"Listen, I get your point, but do I tell you how to take pictures?"

"What? What does that have to do with anything?"

"You have your area of expertise, and I have mine. I've seen what can go wrong with the best-laid plans, when we send in civilian volunteers with wire taps, Kevlar and a SWAT team backing them up and things can still go wrong. It's never predictable."

"But here we are, walking around trying to get him to notice us. Isn't that just as dangerous?"

"Not with me standing here with you."

She had to smile, knowing she was beating her head against a wall, but she really liked the wall, so it was hard to fault him.

"Okay, but can we duck in here? I have to use the ladies' room," she said, nodding to the diner they were passing.

"Sure. I could use a little something anyway."

"We just had lunch a while ago."

"Man needs to eat, and I'm curious about knish…I saw someone order them yesterday and they looked good."

Lacey laughed, and offered a kiss as they found a booth. "I'll make a New Yorker out of you yet," she vowed, heading to the ladies' room.

On her way out of the bathroom, she stopped to check her phone to make sure she hadn't missed any calls, and stiffened as the hairs on the back of her neck stood—someone was right behind her.

Something hard and sharp was pressing into her back, and coldness ran over her skin, chasing away anything but panic and numbing fear as the point dug in.

He'd found her.

JAROD LOOKED AT THE CLOCK. He knew women could take a few minutes in the bathroom, but his instincts were buzzing. Something was wrong. Cursing and throwing some money on the table just as the waitress brought the food he'd ordered for himself and Lacey, he got up and made his way to the back.

Dammit, he should have known. She was right. Myers had waited for her to be alone—and Jarod had let his guard down, thinking they were safe. He should have known better.

Striding along the narrow hallway, he knew he was right as he saw Lacey's sunglasses thrown recklessly on the floor. He picked them up, pushing down the fury and tangle of emotions that threatened to cloud his thinking.

Spotting something else out of the corner of his eye, he saw her lipstick—he knew it was hers, recognizing the case she'd used earlier in the day—lying on the floor near the back door of the diner. She was leaving him a trail, and he just hoped he was in time.

LACEY DIDN'T KNOW what was going on. The man who had her clearly wasn't Scott, and that had rattled her more than if it had been her ex. She struggled, having taken a self-defense course when she moved to the city, and she knew she had to fight for herself. Fighting back was often enough to discourage a would-be attacker.

Luckily her bag was open as she'd left the bathroom, and she'd been dropping stuff left and right, but there was no telling if anyone would notice.

"Just take my bag. There's cash and credit cards, and you can…"

"Shut up, and keep walking." The voice was smooth, almost polished in her ear, his breath warm, but there was the lingering odor of something. As he tightened his grip and she lifted her foot to try to stomp down, pulling at his arms or trying to angle her head so she could bite, she felt the sharp point against the side of her neck and froze. "I don't want your money. I want your man."

"What are you talking about?"

"You be a good girl, you might just make it out of this. It's not you I want, so I don't care if he finds you alive or dying, as long as he comes after you. You should keep that in mind," the soft voice warned.

Her mind finally comprehended his words—she wasn't being mugged or robbed or attacked. At least, not in the way she thought. She was bait.

"Who are you?"

"An old friend of your Ranger's… He's taken something I want back, and he'll tell me where to find it as long as I have something he wants. You," he said and she could hear the smile in his voice, shuddering from revulsion as he buried his head in her neck and sniffed.

"You smell good. Maybe we could have some fun after the Ranger's dead."

"I thought you said you just wanted something from him?"

She had to keep him talking. Maybe someone would hear, she thought, her eyes traveling up the narrow brick walls of the alley behind the diner. The windows were small and high, and if she screamed to get attention, he'd strike. Of that she had no doubt.

"I do. And I plan to get it. And then I plan to make sure he can't follow me where I'm going. Though I have to thank you for dropping things out of your purse to lead him to us—that was helpful," the man said, laughing against her hair.

Her stomach flipped. She'd inadvertently led Jarod into danger. How could he know that this maniac was after him and not her? The man who held her had all the advantages.

"What did he take that you want back?"

"My daughter."

"Jarod won't give you what you want, not even for me."

"Jarod won't give you what you want," he mimicked her in a high-pitched tone, laughing again. "You had better pray that he will. But maybe you like dangerous men? Maybe you like the excitement?" he said seductively, and she held back a cry as his free hand snaked around and covered her breast.

It had been about a minute, and it seemed like a year. Her logical thoughts seemed to have been replaced by fear and hopelessness. Maybe Jarod thought she'd ditched him? Maybe he'd never gone to look for her, or he missed her path of dumped items, or he just couldn't find her, and she was going to die, and probably suffer worse, here in a back alley at the hands of a criminal.

"Darren Hill." The name popped to her lips—the man Jarod had had to identify, the one who had escaped custody in Texas.

"How do you know who I am?" he asked, pressing the knife harder against her throat, and she realized her error. If she knew who he was, he'd never let her walk away.

"My name is Lacey," she said, not answering his question, hoping to buy herself more time.

"So the Ranger told you about me, Lacey. I'm flattered," he said, laughing one moment, and gripping her even harder the next. His tone was angry. "Where the hell are you, Ranger?" he shouted into the alley. "You're sure taking your time, and I might just decide to enjoy myself a little more with your girl here," he said, his hand digging into her tender flesh as she whimpered.

His tone softened again. "You call him. You tell him how you feel with my hands on you, and you beg him to save you," he said and jerked her backward. *"Now."*

"J-Jarod," she called, her voice weak, and then she repeated it more strongly, praying that someone heard if not Jarod. "Jarod—I'm okay. Do what you have to and shoot this sonofabitch between the eyes if you c—"

"Puta!" Hill spat, and pushed her to the ground. The wind was knocked out of her, but she managed to keep from hitting her head. He towered over her, pulling a gun out from his jacket and she froze as he aimed it at her and then both of them were distracted by another voice. Jarod stepped forward out of the converging alley.

Lacey forgot her stone-cold fear, unable to see anything except for her captor swinging the gun in Jarod's direction. White-hot anger took hold and all her walls of fear came crashing down with blind rage. She lashed out, knowing this time she was going to win.

JAROD HEARD THE ECHO of voices and a muffled struggle as he made his way along the alley. Backup was coming, but it wouldn't be here soon enough. The alleys merged and his head snapped up when he heard Lacey's cry, then her shout. He rushed to turn the corner just in time to see Hill shove her to the ground and pull his gun. Jarod shouted instinctively to draw Hills attention his way as he reached for his gun, but Hill had the jump.

He wasn't prepared to see Darren Hill, and he certainly wasn't prepared for what came next.

Lacey, yelling loudly, blindly grabbed onto a bottle lying near a garbage can and swung hard at Darren's crotch, nailing him perfectly. Darren's gun went off, ricocheting wildly around the brick and pavement. Jarod saw him lunge for Lacey, and called out a warning as she skittered away, but then Darren's body arched in surprise and fell to the ground. He groaned in pain. Jarod saw two of New York's finest in an upper window, and three more charging down the alley.

He raced toward where Lacey sat, staring at Darren, who was cursing a blue streak. The NYPD officers dealt with him while Jarod helped Lacey to her feet.

"You okay?" he asked as he searched her for serious injury. The short question was all he could manage as the emotions needed to stay at bay for the moment.

She looked at him steadily and nodded. "Good."

One of the officers approached Jarod. "This the guy you were looking for?"

Jarod nodded, exchanging looks with Hill, who was now cuffed and put in an upright position against the wall while being read his rights, an ambulance screaming in the background.

Turning back to Lacey, he looked her over again, making sure all was well.

"It wasn't Scott," she said to him, sounding confused.

"No. I have to admit, I never seriously thought Darren would have come after me here."

And with that bit of miscalculation, he'd put Lacey in danger. Had almost gotten her killed. Something cold settled down in his gut as he watched the paramedics escort her to the ambulance to check her out, a cop close behind her.

Someone shook him out of his haze, as well, and he realized Lacey was being asked to give a statement. He went with her, keeping a close eye.

She was holding up well, all things considered, and he was proud of her. One tough cookie, his photographer. If not for hitting Hill with that bottle Jarod knew he might be dead.

"Wait—how come you're here now and not over there?" he said, signaling the paramedic, but Lacey grabbed his arm, stopping him.

"They looked me over, and I'm fine. Just some dents and bruises," she joked, even smiled, but he didn't laugh, his gaze focused on her. His hand came up to hold her face.

"You should go to the hospital. I can come with you," he offered.

Her hand covered his. "I'm fine, Jarod. Really. Please, the last thing I need is one more hospital visit."

"He hurt you," Jarod said softly, and touched the bandage at her neck, noticed the bruises.

"Yes, but he won't be able to do that again," she said, stepping closer. "You saved my life. I don't know how you thank someone for that, but—"

"I put you in danger," he said gruffly, still scrutinizing her injuries.

"What?" She was incredulous.

"Tom told me there was a chance Hill would head this way. If he had—"

She put her arms around him, squeezing tightly. "But he didn't. I'm *fine*."

Tenderness that threatened to swallow him whole took hold, and he had to suck a deep breath just to speak.

"Nice shot with the bottle, by the way."

"I know," she said, shaking her head. "After having that scumbag touch me, threaten me, and then he turned that gun on you, I just… Something gave way. No how was he going to win."

"Most people would have let the fear get to them," he said, knowing it was true, and how extraordinary she was.

"I know it probably doesn't make sense, but I feel…good. Really gross, from this alley, and a little sore, but…better than I have in a long time."

"It's the adrenaline, and the relief," Jarod said, wishing he could say the same. She'd apparently faced some demons and put them to rest, but his had just awakened.

Regardless of her disclaimers, she never would have

been in danger if it hadn't been for him, his work, his past. Who was he to think of a future with this woman, any woman? And children, or a life…the kinds of things that men like Darren Hill could hold against him, threaten him with. Unless he stopped being what he was, and that couldn't happen, either.

"Jarod?"

"Huh? Sorry," he said, pushing his hand through his hair.

"Can you please take me home? I'm dirty, and…I just need to be with you right now."

"The hospital—"

"I don't need the hospital. I need you," she said vehemently, and he realized he needed her, too. Needed to forget all the problems and all the reasons it wouldn't work, couldn't work, and enjoy what time they had. It couldn't be forever, but it would have to be enough.

_12_

SUNDAY PASSED in a haze of sex and sleep, both of them wanting nothing more than to be with the other. Lacey was hesitant to take her clothes off, not wanting Jarod to see where Darren's harsh grip had bruised her, but there was no hiding the fact.

Jarod saw everything, absorbed everything and made it all right. He kissed the bruises, replacing the memories of the felon's hard grip with a lover's warm lips and gentle hands. Their lovemaking was just as passionate, but sweeter than before, and Jarod went from tender and loving to playful and teasing as the morning wore on.

"Sunday rule, nothing serious today. We're not leaving the apartment, and we're not thinking about anything else but us. We'll order in, and just enjoy."

She grinned, playing along. She needed the lightness. They ordered pizzas, drinks, salads and desserts, and leftovers filled the kitchen counters and refrigerator. Her stereo played soft renditions of Norah Jones's tunes in the background, and they'd actually danced in her living room. Naked. It was a first.

There were a lot of firsts with Jarod. At the moment,

they were laughing hysterically as bubbles flew everywhere in her bathroom, both of them barely fitting in her clawfoot tub.

The water was lukewarm as they washed and touched each other until the kidding was chased away by desire, and Lacey turned, poised over him, and took his shaft deep inside as she lay back against his chest.

"I've never had a bath quite like *this* before," she said, her voice catching. His arms came around front to apply fragrant bath gel to a sponge before he started sweeping it gently, erotically over her thighs, stomach and breasts. Her breath came faster, and she felt his heart slamming in his chest. She pushed her feet against the bottom of the tub, rocking slightly, drawing a moan from them both.

"Can't say I've ever been much of a bubble bath guy, myself," he said huskily, continuing to wash her as he continued to fill her. He thrust up gently in response to her rocking motions, and water sloshed around them and over the tub's edge onto the tile. "But it's definitely an experience I'd like to repeat."

"Can you repeat that little thing you just did with the sponge?" she asked breathlessly. Her head dropped back when he did, pressing the rough-textured sponge down between her thighs and drawing slowly upward. He applied the right pressure, and she gasped, sensation cascading through her as he leaned down and found her mouth with his, swallowing her cries of release.

As her orgasm spent itself, rippling through her muscles much like the warm water did around her, she planted her hands on the side of the tub. Lifting herself up just enough, she drove down on him harder, then again, knowing what he needed.

"Oh, yeah…like that, just like that," he said, groaning his approval as she complied, his hands splaying over her hips and supporting her and helping her balance. "You're so damned tight…I love when you squeeze me hard inside," he panted, knowing it excited her when he told her what he liked.

His excitement was hard to deny when after only a few more hard thrusts he grabbed her hips and held her down, with a long, guttural sound that told her exactly how satisfied he was.

She wasn't sure she could get enough of him. Her body should be sated, but hearing him come, feeling him come, had her worked up all over again. She was almost embarrassed to admit it, but somehow he knew, and reached down with his hand instead of the sponge and stroked her to a quick, mindless climax that had her trembling.

Getting out, he grabbed a big towel and dried her limp, well-loved form and carried her back to bed. They slept for a while, ate cold pizza, and couldn't help but be aware that the day was ticking to an end, and tomorrow would have to be dealt with.

She woke first, sometime in the middle of the night, and watched him sleep. Tomorrow was their last day working together, and they hadn't said a single word about what came after that.

"Deep thoughts going around in that pretty head?" he murmured, surprising her. She hadn't known he was awake.

"A few."

"Want to share?"

"I'm thinking about tomorrow. The shoot is on the walkways of the Brooklyn Bridge. And then we're done." She paused. "Um, with the calendar shots, I mean. Not… Oh, crap. Never mind."

She closed her eyes, rolling to her back and hitting herself in the forehead quietly with her fist. She was no good at this. She'd never been in this position before, caring so deeply, wanting so much, and not knowing how to navigate the territory between them.

"Hey." He grabbed her hand. "No beating yourself in the head. Didn't we talk about that?" he teased.

She laughed lightly. "I feel like I'm thirteen with the boy I like and completely flubbing it."

"You like me, huh?"

"Yeah. I do like you."

"I like you, too."

"I noticed."

"But there are a few things in the way," Jarod spoke calmly. "Namely, my job is a risky one. I grew up watching my mother suffer, wondering if Dad was coming home from work every day until she couldn't take it anymore. I swore I'd never do that to anyone. When Hill took you…I realized what a mistake I'd made."

Her heart hammered. It was dark and she could barely make out his silhouette as he looked at her. "This isn't a mistake."

"No, this isn't, but starting to fall in love with you is. Thinking about dragging you into my life is—Hill might not be the last, or the worst. I don't want you to suffer like my mom did, always wondering, only to watch what we have now implode."

Lacey blinked, fully awake, and pushed herself up on the mattress. *Love*. He'd said he was starting to fall in love with her.

He continued, "When I saw him holding the gun over you, and knew I was responsible for that…it's something I can't live with."

She pulled back a bit. "And I have nothing to say in the matter?"

She heard the coolness in her own voice, but couldn't help it. She understood his fears, but wasn't he the one who was telling her that you couldn't let fear run your life?

"It's not that…it's just, well, sweetheart, you've been through enough, and—"

"Don't," she said quietly.

"What? Don't what?"

"Don't think about me that way. It's why I never wanted anyone to know what happened to me in the first place, and I thought you were…you were the exception."

"I don't know what you're talking about, Lacey," he said, turning on a light and sounding frustrated.

"You're turning me into a victim—some person who can't make their own choices, like someone who needs to be shielded and protected."

"Of course you can make your own choices, and I don't see you as a victim, not in the way you mean. In both cases, you fought back, saving yourself, and even saving me," he said, meeting her eyes, and she felt some of the tension dissolve. "But I do want to protect you. I can't help it, it's who I am. But what about the time that I can't? What about the next nutcase or freak out for revenge that—"

"Then I guess you trust me to handle it myself and hope for the best," she interrupted, reaching up to touch his face.

He was so handsome, but that wasn't the thing that made her heart contract inside her chest. He touched her more deeply than she thought anyone could. "I'm falling for you, too, but there's no need to rush things. We have time," she reassured him, suddenly finding herself in the position of quelling his fears.

Everything inside of her warmed when he smiled.

"You're an amazing woman, you know that?"

"I suspected," she said teasingly, and they laughed, but then he became serious again.

"I don't know, Lacey. I always said I'd never put anyone in the same position my mom was in, and I have this good shot at a promotion, even though the pictures we lost, uh—"

"What about the pictures?" Her senses sharpened. "Did those pictures show up somewhere?"

"My captain got them, yeah."

She slid down to the mattress again, staring at the ceiling.

"You didn't tell me."

"You had enough to worry about, and it wasn't an issue. Tom is my captain, but he's also a friend, and he knew what was going on—he brushed them for prints, but whoever it was, was careful."

"It could have cost you your job."

"Not really. Well, it might have raised some eyebrows, but I technically wasn't on duty, and there's nothing unethical about me being involved with you, so except for making it somewhat awkward, I don't know what anyone hoped to gain by sending them. I would have thought they'd send them to your bosses."

"If they did, I never heard a word about it."

She could see the cop emerge as he slipped into pensive mode.

"So maybe someone was trying to piss me off, to get me to have to leave, to separate us…to leave you unprotected?"

She sighed. They were back to that.

"I suppose, but why force issues? You'd be going home eventually anyway."

"That's true. I don't know. None of it makes sense." He leaned over, planted a hot kiss on her lips. "I'm sorry I didn't tell you, but honestly, at the time, it didn't seem like the most important thing. And I didn't want you to worry."

"You know, if we stay in this, if we make this…more, then I will worry. How could I not? But I don't think that's a reason for us not to be together," she said, then frowned. "We have more practical problems."

"Such as?"

"Well, the fact that we live in two pretty distant places, and we're both building careers, that are kind of geographically challenging?"

He sighed. "I know. I've tried to find a way around it, too."

"I don't know what will happen after the calendar is done. I might stay here, I could be back on freelance, and that sends me all over the place for varying amounts of time. What was the promotion you were mentioning?"

His fingers started trailing up and down her arm, and she shivered, but not from cold.

"Tom is moving up, and wants me to take his spot. It's a test, some interviews, but he thinks I'd get the job. It's more desk time, more office work—"

She snorted. "That doesn't sound like you at all. Why would you even consider it?"

"I don't know. Better pay, more regular hours, less chance of dying out in the desert. The basics, really."

He joked, but what she knew in her heart was that he was considering it for her, for them. And it was too much—too much that he'd consider such a sacrifice when they'd only known each other for a week and couldn't predict how things would be a week from now.

She sighed, reaching up and pulling him down next to her, and he didn't argue, leaning in to trail kisses over her face and neck, moving down to her stomach.

"Let's just take it a day at a time, okay? Can we not make any big decisions? Let's just…enjoy this," she said, sucking in a breath as his lips closed around her nipple and drew sweetly on the sensitive bud.

"Fine by me," he whispered, his breath feathering over the spot his mouth had made wet, creating more sensation.

Levering over her, he parted her thighs with his

shoulders and settled in, kissing her intimately, laving her soft flesh with his tongue until she was writhing and begging for him to fill her, a command he was happy to follow.

Settling down on top of her slender form, he entered her gently. He rained kisses down her neck, her chest while he moved slowly and tantalizingly back and forth, rocking them to a climax that had them both shuddering in each other's arms.

Later, as dawn peeked over the windowsill of her apartment, they looked at each other quietly and made no promises. How they touched each other was promise enough for now.

JAROD TURNED HIS GAZE from the view of Lower Manhattan, to the people setting up his last bunch of shots. Oddly, he no longer felt strange being made up, his clothes changed, as he got ready for the shoot. Maybe it was because anything that allowed him to be close to Lacey right now was okay with him.

"Did you know the Brooklyn Bridge is the only place on earth where an airplane can fly overhead while you are walking over a car that is driving over a boat that is floating over a train?" she asked with a smile, camera in hand.

After their talk last night, they hadn't mentioned any future plans again, but he still was uncomfortable leaving her until everything was settled. He'd promised he wouldn't, but work demands dictated his presence back home. He was being asked to travel with a marshall to bring Hill back to Texas, and it wouldn't wait.

Jarod smiled, wanting to pull her close, but resisting, as they were on work time. "I hadn't thought of that before. Makes me consider the people who built all of this. Utterly amazing."

"I'm always freaked out by the pictures of the men sitting on the girders back in the twenties, eating their lunch—no ropes, nothing attaching them. Incredible."

"A lot of lives lost over the decades, building this place," he said, his eyes drifting back to the island.

"Yes, but as much happiness, too, I'd like to think."

"Is that why you came here? To find happiness?"

She took a deep breath. "No. I wasn't even thinking about happiness, then." She studied him from under her lashes, blushing slightly before turning her gaze out over the river. "I came here to escape. It was far enough away, big enough, and different enough, and I thought no one could find me here. I guess I was wrong."

"People have gone to the desert for exactly the same reason. They're really not all that different in the basic sense—both big and threatening if you don't know your way around, and both beautiful."

"You have some poetry in you, Ranger," she teased, turning when someone called to her.

"We're all set. Ready to make love to the camera, stud?"

"Always ready to make love to the woman handling it," he said just as playfully, loving her smile.

She hadn't done the things other women might have done. She didn't pressure him to stay, or complain that he had to leave, even though he'd wanted to remain until Myers was caught. All in all, she seemed okay with things the way they were. He wasn't as sure that he was.

"There's still no word on Myers or Gena—they don't even know if she's still alive."

"I realize that," she said softly. "But there have been no more calls, no more problems."

"Somehow it seems like if he was here, he would have popped up by now."

"I can't think of anyone else who'd be calling me or who would have broken into my apartment."

Jarod took his position at the bridge railing and leaned back as she fiddled with his shirt and posture.

"Maybe he figured out he couldn't get to you and left. Those guys are basically cowards. They like to exert their power, and when they can't win, they take off."

"I guess. It would make me feel better if they found him, though."

He had to say it. It wasn't the best time, but the words came out. "I know I said I'd be here until we straightened that out, and I don't feel right leaving you, but I don't have a choice."

Her eyes flickered with various emotions, and he knew she wasn't exactly in the best position to talk at the moment, but it had to be said.

"I'll be fine. I'll be careful. I'm going to stay at Jackie's for a few days anyway. She needs help getting home from the hospital tomorrow, and she'll need someone there for a day or two. Maybe by then we'll hear something."

"I'll talk to a cop here who I've gotten to know a bit. He can stop by, or check things out for you, too."

"Thanks. I'm sure I'll be fine," she said.

"I want to come back as soon as I can swing it, and…I'm not taking the promotion. I talked to Tom this morning."

"Good for you, Ranger," she said approvingly, and not caring who saw, pulled at his collar, bringing him down for a quick kiss, to his surprise. "Now look pretty for the pictures," she ordered, joining her crew who had discreetly averted their eyes.

"Very funny," he replied, but watching her work was fun, and he got through the final shots with ease.

"I'm treating everyone to pizza at Grimaldi's," she announced, and he was disappointed not to have her to himself.

"Pizza sounds great," he agreed and focused on the festive mood as they packed up and made their way from the bridge into Brooklyn, pleased as she snaked her hand into his.

As she said, they had time. He didn't know how, but he knew he wasn't going to let Lacey Graham out of his life, one way or the other.

THE AIRPORT WAS HELL, and Lacey didn't mean the traffic, the crowds or the delays. She'd rented a car to pick up Jackie from the hospital, not wanting to subject her bruised friend to a possibly adventurous cab ride, and take Jarod to the airport, which gave her extra time with him, too.

"You're a good driver," he observed as she made her way off the Expressway heading toward the airport.

"It's been so long since I've driven, I almost forgot if

I could do it. It's actually not quite as bad here as I thought."

They arrived at the airport, and she hadn't anticipated how difficult it would be to say goodbye, even though she knew it was temporary. She'd felt so confident and adult the night before, telling *him* not to worry. And that they'd work things out and find a way to be together. Not to rush things. But now she felt like the neediest Nellie on the planet.

Good Lord, how she didn't want him getting on that plane. She stopped herself short of telling him she didn't want him to go because she was an independent woman, and doing so was clingy and unattractive and—

"God, I wish I didn't have to go," he said roughly, and she bit her lip to hold back the emotion that welled up. He gathered her in close to comfort her.

"I'll be back as soon as I can. I'll come up here until you're done with the calendar, and after that's over, maybe you can take a break and come down to my neck of the woods?"

He gently tipped her chin up and looked into her eyes, and it did her good to know he hated this as much as she did.

"Sounds like a plan," she said, forcing a smile that he scooped up in a hot kiss. He checked his watch and reluctantly pulled back. "You be careful. And call me if you need me. You've got Ward's direct number, too, remember," he said. Ward was the NYPD officer he'd dealt with on the Hill shooting.

"I will. I'll be fine. You stay safe, too," she said, realizing the reality of what he had been talking about as he got out of the car with his bag and walked away.

It was the first moment that she really understood why he had such serious doubts. On a daily basis, Jarod's life could be in danger. They had plans, but it was really a day-by-day thing. Who knew if he'd come back, if she'd ever see him again? He was getting on that plane with a Federal Marshall and the man who had tried to kill them both.

No. She couldn't think that way. Jarod was good at what he did. He'd be back.

Watching him disappear as he entered the aiport, she waited until her vision stopped being so blurry and started the car. She had work, and she had to take care of Jackie. She loved Jarod, but she had her life, too, and she was going to get back to it.

13

"I'M SORRY YOU HAD to miss the pizza wrap-up lunch. It was fun, and I think we got things back on track, so we're off and running again," Lacey said to Jackie as they waited for the nurse to come with a wheelchair. Jackie grumped.

"It's so stupid to have to be wheeled out of these places. I'm perfectly fine to walk. I just want to get home."

"I don't blame you, but enjoy the rest while you're getting it. I'm doubling up the schedule over the next few weeks so we can get more finished. Now that Jarod's pictures are done, and I've got plenty of Ryan and another guy coming in tomorrow, I have a much better idea of what I need from everyone else. We're actually ahead of schedule. I think we can cut through it all much faster, thankfully."

Lacey was particularly motivated to stay on schedule because when she was done she was taking a few weeks off to visit Jarod. That was the advantage of freelance work, and she was going to enjoy it.

"Execs will be happy about that. Nothing like being on track," Jackie said and let out a small whoop of happiness when the nurse appeared in the doorway.

"Yay, time to go," her assistant gushed, and Lacey chuckled as they all headed for the entrance. Soon she and Jackie were making their way to Hoboken, where Jackie lived.

"So…how are you doing?" Jackie asked, once she'd settled into her place.

"Me? I'm fine. You're the one recovering."

"You know what I mean. Jarod had to go home, and Sally came in and mentioned to me that you two were pretty hot and heavy at the shoot, not that I didn't know something was going on before. You two could start fires just by looking across a room at each other," Jackie said.

Lacey couldn't help but grin. "He's a great guy."

"C'mon! That's all you're going to give me?" Jackie let her head fall back against the seat's headrest, rolling her eyes in disgust. "I'm an injured woman, I need details."

Lacey laughed again. "Well…he's coming back, maybe in a few weeks, and I'm going there at the end of the project…"

"And?"

"And what?"

"You're killin' me here. What's he like in the sack? What do you like most about him? Are you guys in something serious, or what?"

"We're taking our time—it's only been a week. But I'd say we both agree it could be something serious, and because of that, I'm not telling you about the other stuff. Except to say that I think I pulled several all-nighters in the past week, and I enjoyed every single second of them."

"Yesss!" Jackie said, clapping.

"I know. I never thought there would be a guy like him out there. Decent, sexy, caring... I mean, he has his faults—he's a little bossy, a little, um, not arrogant, but you know, he kind of likes to take over if you let him—"

"Which you don't."

"No, but he listens, too. Even when we disagreed, we could actually talk, and he *heard* what I had to say, you know?"

Jackie didn't say anything, and Lacey looked over as they stopped at a light, seeing her friend sitting, staring down into her lap at her fingers.

"Hey, what's the matter? You feeling all right?"

Jackie sniffed and shook her head. "Yeah, I'm fine. I'm just happy for you. You deserve it."

"How about you and Kenny?"

"I, uh, I don't think it's going to work out."

"I'm sorry to hear that. But take it from me there are many, and better, fish. Maybe that fireman who was flirting with you last week? What was his name? Mr. April. I can remember their month, but forget their names. Except for Jarod, of course."

Jackie smiled weakly. "Ryan Murphy. He was nice. Maybe. Right now, I don't know if I want anything to do with men at all."

Lacey remained quiet for a moment. "I know how you feel. That's where I was before I met Jarod."

"Really?"

"I know it's different, but a man attacked you, Jackie, maybe the same man who attacked me once."

There, she said it.

"Is that what you guys were talking about that day, and why they sent security to my hospital room?"

"That's right. We were afraid he'd come back, that he was trying to get to me through my friends, through Jarod—he sent the pictures of us to Jarod's boss."

"Oh, no! Is he in trouble?"

"No, it sounds like his captain kept it quiet. Jarod hadn't crossed any ethical lines by being with me. But obviously someone was trying to mess with us. Maybe make him think I was too much trouble, or get him to leave." Lacey shrugged.

"You said you were attacked, too?"

"My ex-boyfriend was a maniac, and beat me before he took off. It was why I came here, and it ate away at me until I settled some things recently, I guess."

Jackie's voice was thin. "He hit you?"

"He broke my arm, threw me around… I think he might have done worse if I hadn't passed out."

"Oh, my God," Jackie said. "I'm so sorry."

Lacey felt a knot loosen in her gut. This was easier to talk about than she thought, and it felt good to get it out, especially as maybe it could help Jackie.

"Thing is, I didn't want to deal with it or talk to anyone. I told Jarod, and you, and somewhere in all of it, I started to work through it. That's my point, really. You were hurt, too, and you might need to talk about it, or do something to get past it. Just don't lock it up inside like I did because it eats at you. It doesn't go away on its own."

Jackie said nothing, and Lacey worried. It was so

unlike Jackie to be so quiet or moody, but then again, she'd been through so much recently.

"Jackie, I'm sorry if you didn't need to hear all that right now. I know I hated people preaching at me to talk about it, or to tell someone… I had to come around to it in my own good time, so I'm sorry I pushed."

Jackie shook her head. "It's not that."

"We're almost there. Just relax, okay?"

"Lacey, there's something I really need to tell you," Jackie started, but Lacey inadvertently cut her off when someone cut her off, taking a turn far too fast.

"Damn, that guy nearly took our front end off! What were you about to say?"

"Um, nothing, maybe later. Thanks for telling me all this. Do you really think it was the same guy?"

"I don't know. I really have no idea anymore what's going on. Things have been calm for a few days, and so Jarod thought maybe Scott went away. You didn't see him?"

Jackie went back to looking out the window.

"Well, listen, we'll keep each other company, and we'll be perfectly safe. And if you want, I can even grab more stuff from my place and keep you company for a few days."

"You don't have to do that."

"It's what friends do for each other, Jackie, and I hope we are friends."

"I hope we are, too."

"Okay, here we are. Where can I park?"

Jackie directed her to a space on the street, and Lacey helped her out of the car, noticing a pizza place close by, her heart squeezing a little. Ordinary as it might be, pizza was now kind of a special thing, having been the first date she had with Jarod, even if she hadn't thought of it that way at the time.

"That place serves a piece of pizza almost as big as a whole pie—they're kind of known for it. There's a great bagel shop, as well. Kinda funky," Jackie said, noticing her staring down the street.

They made their way up to the teeny third-floor apartment, and Lacey was delighted to find that there was a roof garden and a patio accessible from Jackie's loft.

"This is so cute! I should look for a place over here, if I stay in the city long-term."

"It is nice—quieter, more like a small town, in some ways. Nice neighbors."

They settled in, and Lacey went out to bring back a couple of the huge pizza slices, figuring Jackie might need a few minutes alone. She was acting a little strangely, and Lacey knew she just had to be patient, and be a friend. It was something she'd been lacking after her own ordeal.

Returning up the building's steps, she realized that in a few weeks, she'd developed more close relationships than she had in months before, just by opening up. She didn't feel alone anymore, and the future looked brighter than it had in a long while.

LACEY WAS EXHAUSTED and slightly uncomfortable on Jackie's sofa. She missed Jarod and figured being here on the lumpy couch was better than being home alone in her bed. She jumped when her phone rang, hoping it was him.

"Hello?"

"Hey, sweetheart, you awake?"

"Yes, I was just reading and missing you like crazy. Good flight?"

"Boring. Long. The usual. But they got Hill where they needed him to be, and tomorrow it's business as usual for me. I miss you, too."

"I take it there's been no information on Scott?" she asked.

"Nothing. He seems to have evaporated. Maybe he went over the border, who knows? A friend of mine said it wouldn't be typical of his profile to come back after you, so that's a comfort, I guess."

"Although it doesn't explain any of the stuff that has been happening."

"You alone there?"

"Jackie's in the next room, sleeping, though her TV is on. Why?"

She smiled to herself, able to tell from the tone of his voice that something was on his mind—something sexy, for sure.

"Because just hearing your voice is turning me on, and I figured, since we're giving this long-distance thing a shot, we'll have to get creative once in a while. Are you feeling creative?"

"Sure, but let me get to a more private spot. There's a nice patio on the roof, I can go up there. It's a little muggy outside, but I'm feeling kind of hot anyway," she said teasingly, and heard him groan appreciatively.

Making her way up the steep metal fire escape steps to the roof, she was relieved to discover that she was alone. Her heart picked up a little as she contemplated what she and Jarod might say to each other with her sitting out here in the open.

"It's gorgeous up here, Jarod. They even planted a small patch of lawn on half of the roof, with flower boxes and benches, a swing and a grill. I guess everyone uses it, the eight people who rent here."

"So that means you could get caught." His tone was low and naughty. "Does that bother you?"

"Not really…I can be discreet."

She could hardly believe that she was getting breathless from just talking to him about sex. Although she had a feeling it was going to go a lot further than talk very shortly.

"Where are you sitting? The bench or the swing?"

"The swing. It looked inviting and has a canopy. The cushion is soft and I can stretch out. In fact, it's pretty warm outside, so I think I'm going to lose my top, do you mind?"

Another groan. "Are you seriously taking off your shirt?"

She had a very sturdy running bra on underneath, but Jarod didn't need to know that, she decided with wicked glee.

"I am, and I did. There's a soft breeze, and my nipples are very hard because I'm hearing your voice, and thinking about your mouth," she said, and that much was true. She was already on fire for him.

"I thought I was supposed to be seducing you," he said roughly, but with a laugh.

"You are. You tell me anything you want me to do,

or what you'd do to me if you were here…and I'll do the same," she instructed, loving this new way to play.

"You know I love it when you talk dirty, sweetheart, so don't hold back."

"I don't intend to. All I've been thinking about is how I'd like to—"

A sharp noise from below her made her stop and frown.

"Lacey?"

"I'm sorry—I heard a loud noise, and it sounded like it came from directly below, which would be Jackie's room."

"You should go check. Keep me on the line."

"Okay," she agreed, and heard another loud bang, along with a yelp, and moved faster. "Jarod, something's wrong. I think I just heard her scream."

"Lacey, stop! Forget it, don't go in there. Get off the line and call for help, but stay out of there, okay?"

"Okay," she said, hanging up and dialing 911 at the top of the steps, but as she heard another cry, she flinched and peeped around the edge of the door leading to the escape, and saw Jackie's apartment door flung open.

She quickly gave the emergency operator the info and moved carefully down the steps. She had to see if she could help. If Jackie was already hurt, and in there alone, Lacey wouldn't forgive herself if all she'd done was just wait outside.

Sliding along the wall, she saw an older lady down the hall poke her head out and yell, "What the hell is going on down there?"

Lacey put her finger to her lips and frantically motioned her back inside. The woman glared, and muttered something, but ducked inside her door. Probably to call the police. Fine—the more the merrier.

It was silent in the apartment. Not a good sign, and Lacey stopped just outside the door. Suddenly assailed by a million doubts, she wondered if she was really going to be able to help Jackie, or if she was making a horrible error in judgment.

She took a deep breath. Too late now. She stepped into the apartment, pushing the door back and saw nothing, but then heard a noise from the bedroom.

Jackie.

Heart slamming in her chest, Lacey reached out and grabbed a baseball bat Jackie kept by the door—she called it her "burglar bat," which Lacey had found funny at the time. Now, the solid wood felt good in her hands. It was something.

Moving farther in, she heard papers shuffling, and a drawer closing. Could this be a robbery? There was no way Scott could know she was here, unless he had followed them.

She failed to breathe when her ringtone chimed from her pocket and she realized she hadn't shut her cell phone off. It had to be Jarod calling back.

Shit.

She turned, heading for the door, but didn't quite make it.

14

"Whoa there, honey. You hold up. And you can put down that bat, too," commanded a male voice she didn't recognize. It was an inebriated male voice, as well. She could tell from the slurring of his words.

She faced a tall blond man who looked rough around the edges and didn't fit her idea of a burglar at all. Her phone stopped ringing, and went to voice mail. Jarod must be crazed, she imagined, but she didn't have time to worry about that now.

"Like hell I will. Where's Jackie?" Lacey asked calmly, and noted the man's eyes flare.

"She shouldn't-a brought you here…she knows how you piss me off. She told me to get lost. Do you believe that? Picked you over me," he said with incredulity, his gaze turning mean. "But I showed her."

Lacey then realized whom she was talking to.

"Kenny? You're Jackie's boyfriend?"

"I was…until the ungrateful bitch dumped me, refused to keep helping me get what I deserved."

Lacey heard a soft moan from the other room, behind Kenny, and homed in on his words.

"How was Jackie helping you do that?"

"She was helping me get to you, you know? I asked her to mess up a few things. Just enough to make you look bad, but she wasn't doing a good job, so I had to *help*," he said, throwing his hands up, which made Lacey jump. And he laughed more loudly.

"Why would you want me off the project?"

He shoved his hand in his pocket and pulled out a wad of paper. "See this? This is the list. She wouldn't give it to me before, she said she was going to tell you it was me, turn me in."

"So you took it and put her in the hospital? It was you?"

"Dumb bitch," he muttered. "You're all bitches. You come in from wherever, flashing your tits and your baby blues and get whatever you want. Do you know how long I have worked in this stupid city, barely scraping by, and you just walk right in?"

"That's not my fault, and it's not Jackie's fault, either."

"It is her fault!" he roared, and Lacey fought a cringe, trying to keep him talking. What was taking the police so long? "She was on the inside, she could have put in a word for me, she could have gotten rid of you! She coulda done a million things, but she wouldn't do it, wouldn't help me, she said. Until I made her." He took a knife from his jacket pocket, smiling.

Lacey's mind traveled back along the timeline, remembering Jackie's hand.

Five stitches, Jackie had said, from cutting an onion. Jackie didn't even like onions. She always told the lunch guy to leave them off her sandwich.

"You *cut* her?"

He shrugged. "She had to learn not to say no to me when I needed her. Not to put some bitch at work above her man, or there would be consequences. The cut was just enough to get the message across. I could do much worse. Wanna see?"

He waved the knife and Lacey felt a shiver run down her body. It had blood on it.

Oh, God. Jackie....

She raised the bat, more afraid than she ever had been, and looked him in the eye. She wasn't taking any chances.

Where are the cops?

"What did you do, you lousy, cowardly sonofabitch?" she growled at him. He wiggled his eyebrows, grinning madly.

"Weeha, you have some spunk, don't you? This will be fun," he said with relish, swiping the knife in an arc and moving from one foot to the other. Lacey moved quickly and put a chair between them, a wall at her back, and held the bat poised.

"I've called the police, and so did the lady next door," she spat, hoping the latter was true. "They'll be here any minute. You'll never make it out of here."

"Aw, this won't take more than a minute," he teased. "I'm so sick of rich, privileged bitches taking everything from the people who work hard for it. Let's see how well you do in the world if your face ain't so pretty."

The world whittled down to just the small space containing the two of them. He moved closer, swinging and feinting, laughing again, and Lacey held the bat high. She heard sirens wail and car doors slam, but the sounds seemed far away.

Kenny's face was fierce as he came closer, moving faster, and she might have screamed, but wasn't sure. He looked to the side, distracted by something, and she took her chance, swinging forward, fast and hard.

Home freakin' run.

She wasn't aiming for anything specifically, but hit him somewhere in the gut. The knife went flying, someone shouted, and Kenny fell to the floor with a grunt.

He started to get back up, and Lacey drew the bat high a second time, but someone grabbed it and people crowded her vision. She fought to free herself, her eyes trained on Kenny.

"Calm down, ma'am, it's okay. Lacey? Calm down. We're here, and we've got him."

She dared to take her eyes from Kenny when she realized officers had entered the room, the one next to her holding the bat with one hand, waiting for her to recognize him.

"Officer Ward," she said, remembering the name from Jarod, and he nodded.

"That's me. How about you relax now? We've got him," he said.

"My friend…Jackie, she's in there," she cried, tears, relief and adrenaline all hitting at once. "She's hurt…he hurt her, again. He attacked her before. He—he cut her hand…"

Suddenly her phone rang and the cop in front of her glanced toward her pocket.

"I think that's for you. Why don't you answer it, and then we'll take a statement, okay?"

She nodded, reaching for her phone, watching two

other officers drag Kenny from the room as he cursed left and right.

She put the phone to her ear, looking toward Jackie's room, where police had gone in but hadn't come out. She could hardly breathe as the paramedics raced into the apartment. She pointed and they went into Jackie's room, too.

"Lacey? Is that you? You're there?"

Jarod's voice broke through the fog.

"I'm here. I'm...okay."

"Oh, God, honey, you near gave me a heart attack when you didn't answer the phone. What the hell is happening?"

She started to tell him, but then she saw Jackie being wheeled out by the paramedics. Lacey ran to her side, so happy to see her eyes open.

"Jackie," she whispered, taking her hand as they wheeled her through the apartment.

Jackie looked at her but didn't respond. She tried to say something Lacey thought might have been "sorry" but she couldn't tell.

Jarod was saying something, asking what was happening. Lacey told him she was there, asked the paramedics if Jackie was okay.

"Lacey, goddammit, what—"

Lacey fell into a chair, her knees trembling. "It's okay, Jarod. It was Kenny, Jackie's boyfriend. He was doing it all, the pictures, the apartment, the fires, the calls... He wanted the calendar project. He made her help. He was the one who hurt her."

"Is Jackie okay?"

"He came after her, but I guess I interrupted him doing anything really bad, and so, yeah, she'll be okay. Physically. He's done a job on her mentally. I don't understand…I never would have guessed. She never showed any sign of a problem like this, but maybe I wasn't paying attention."

"You saved her life. And risked your own, which we are going to have a long talk about…"

She smiled, and started to laugh and cry at the same time. "There's a policeman here who wants to talk to me, Jarod."

"Okay. Do what you have to. Remember I love you."

It was the first time he'd said it just like that, and it put the world to rights.

"I love you, too," she said, meaning it. "I'll call you back as soon as we're done."

"Promise?"

"Promise."

JAROD LEFT LACEY a message, unable to wait for her to call back. Talking on the phone just wasn't going to cut it. He had to be there.

Turning around almost as soon as he'd gotten home, he got a ridiculously expensive last-minute business flight and took off. Five hours later, the sun was just short of coming up, and he was jumping out of a cab in front of Lacey's apartment. He was nearly crazy with the need to see her, touch her, and make sure she was okay.

She opened the door to his furious knocking, sleepy-eyed and standing there wearing a shirt—his shirt that he left behind, and he couldn't get her in his arms fast enough. Closing the door behind him, he pulled her in tight, running his hands over her, making sure everything really was all right.

When he finally loosened his hold and she looked up, he just captured her mouth in a kiss, soaking in her touch, her scent, her taste, even though it had only been a little more than twelve hours since he had last seen her.

"I had to be here. I shouldn't have left in the first place," he said against her mouth, now starting to believe that she really was okay.

Lacey shook her head, making some utterly female, comforting noise that wrapped right around his heart.

"I can't believe you came back. Did you get any sleep at all?"

"I don't need sleep. Like I could sleep. Do you have any idea what it felt like to hear you and know that you were in danger, and to not be there? The things that went through my mind, sweetheart, when you didn't pick up that phone—"

"I'm sorry. I just… I couldn't let Jackie be hurt. It was rough, but it worked out okay."

"You could have been killed," he said flatly.

She nodded. "Twice in a week, that must be some kind of record, even for a New Yorker," she said wryly.

"How can you joke about this? And Myers is still missing. No way am I moving from this spot until he's found."

She moved back, looking partly amused, partly turned on, and partly consternated.

"Jarod, you can't do that. You have your job, re-member? The one you are supposed to report to in—" she slid a look to the clock "—about an hour?"

"They can fire me."

"Be serious."

"I'm completely serious. In everything I ever faced in the course of my work, I don't think I was ever as afraid as I was when you didn't pick up that phone."

She frowned. "You're focusing on the wrong thing."

"What?"

Sitting on the sofa and pulling her lovely legs up under her, she yawned and patted the seat next to her. He went and sat close, his fingers finding her nape and stroking the silky hair there, still needing to touch her and reassure himself she was okay.

"You're focusing on the problem, on the fact that you weren't here to protect me, but what you aren't focusing on is that I was able to protect myself," she said with a sort of fierce look in her eye that surprised Jarod, but shouldn't have.

"I know. I know that. Rationally," he said. "But in here—" he took her hand and put it up against his heart "—I wanted to be the one to make sure you're safe. That you don't ever have to do that, ever again. I don't know how I can do that with us far apart. Or how my job figures in, or what I—"

She shook her head. "You can't. You have to be who you are, and let me be who I am, and we just have to have faith it will be okay. Seeing what Jackie went through with Kenny, and realizing I could have helped sooner, I could have maybe avoided the entire thing—"

"Wait—how? You aren't to blame here."

"No, not to blame, exactly. I know it's Kenny's fault. But I was so wrapped up in my own issues, wanting to hide and pretend nothing had ever happened to me, that I couldn't see what was happening to someone standing right in front of me. Maybe if I had…opened up, you know, gone to the counseling, allowed myself to heal sooner, Jackie would have told me what was happening to her."

"That's a lot of maybes. How is she doing?"

"She's okay."

Lacey looked down, taking a breath, her words coming out quickly, as if she had to muster the courage to say them.

"I'm going to go talk to someone later—an abuse counselor—to work through my own stuff, but also hoping it will encourage Jackie to do the same."

Jarod felt his own throat tighten and swallowed hard. "You are the bravest woman I have ever known in my life, I swear," he said huskily, bringing her fingers to his lips.

"You helped me get there. You made me believe again," she said, and he knew no matter what the hardships, they couldn't abandon what they had. They'd just find a way to make it work.

Pulling her up against him, he kissed her more lazily this time, his tongue touching hers in a slow, mating motion. His body reacted sharply with relief and desire as she pressed into him wearing nothing but the shirt.

"Let me call Tom and give him the rundown. I'll go

back as soon as I can get a flight out tomorrow but for now maybe we should go to bed for a few hours...get some rest or something," he said, tasting the warm, soft skin of her neck.

"Or something," she agreed, as his large hand massaged her breast.

THE FURTHEST THING from Lacey's mind was sleep. It had taken hours for the adrenaline to wear off. As he touched her intimately, everything inside of her body seemed to melt. In spite of the stress and lack of sleep, she wanted him.

She'd been surprised, though overjoyed, to get his message that he was coming back. The news had kept her awake for hours as she waited to see him again, and to feel his hands on her. However, it didn't look as though either one of them was going to leave the couch until they'd had their fill. She smiled as he unbuttoned the shirt.

It was, of course, the moment her cell phone rang.

"Mmm...might be about Jackie. I asked them to call me," she said, breaking away.

"Answer it. Then meet me in the bedroom."

The words were wickedly delicious coming from him, and she watched him walk away rather than looking at the caller ID on her phone.

Her warm mood and fuzzy feelings crystallized into something cold and sharp when she heard a familiar voice.

"Lacey, don't hang up."

Hang up? She was so stunned she couldn't move.

She tried to breathe normally, her heart hammering as she ran down the hall and grabbed Jarod by the arm, silently mouthing to him who was on the phone.

Like magic, his expression went from molten sexuality to granite. He made a hand motion for her to keep her caller talking and she nodded.

"I'm not hanging up, Scott. How did you find me? Are you in the city?"

Jarod gave her the thumbs-up as he grabbed his own phone.

"That's why I'm calling, I, uh… Gena heard that you were having a bad time with someone, and they were looking for me, and it's not me. I'm calling to say I'm, uh, sorry. But I haven't been following you. I've changed, Lacey, or at least, I'm trying to."

"I know it wasn't you, Scott, but that doesn't explain why you're calling me. The restraining order is still—"

"Listen, I'm in love with Gena. I took off because I needed to get to her, not to come after you. We had a fight, and I was locked up in that house. She wouldn't answer my calls, so I had to risk going to find her."

Lacey's blood ran cold. "Is Gena okay? Did you hurt her?"

"Hurt her? No! I would never hurt her. She's here with me. She's the one who told me to call you. I…wanted to say I'm sorry for what happened, for what I did to you. Part of it was the drugs, the booze, but my counselors said I can't use that as an excuse, and they're right."

Lacey listened, and felt more or less as if she'd fallen down the rabbit hole.

"Scott, I don't know what game you're playing, but

you'd be better off to turn yourself in. At the very least, you've broken house arrest."

"I know. I had to do it. When I told her I'd taken off, she met me here and told me to turn myself in. I guess I'll have to do extra time, but maybe if I give myself up, they'll let me finish at home in L.A."

She grabbed a pen and wrote "Reno" on the pad. Jarod started to dial but she motioned for him to stop.

"If you're lying, you should know I'm not alone, and they're looking for you—you won't get away with this."

"I'm not playing games, not anymore. I—I had a lot of problems, and I didn't know how to handle them. I'm learning now. I'm trying."

"If what you're saying is true, and I hope it is, for Gena's sake, then I'll wish you well," she said, feeling something spring loose inside of her. "You can't ever call me again, Scott. You hurt me badly, and I want you out of my life, completely, forever."

"Thanks, Lacey. You'll never hear from me again, I promise."

He hung up, and that was that.

Jarod was on the phone and though she paced for twenty minutes while he checked, eventually he hung up, shaking his head incredulously.

"It's true. He's turned himself in to the Reno police. He says he's in love with Gena. She's there with him, confirming his story. He escaped, called her, and she left to find him, to try to get him to turn himself in."

"He…apologized." The idea hit her as so strange that she couldn't quite get her mind around it yet.

"It gets weirder. They want to get married, so that they could legally see each other while he's finishing his sentence. You okay?"

She nodded. "I just feel…strange. I don't know what I expected, but it wasn't that. I can't really forgive him, but at the same time, I kind of hope he makes it. For her sake, anyway."

"That's a kind of forgiveness…it's healthy, but confusing, I know. I've seen victims forgive their attackers, or those who killed loved ones. I've never been able to imagine doing the same, but they tend to say it sets them free in a way."

Lacey nodded. "Yes…there is that feeling, I think. Like it's finally, really over."

Jarod extended his hand. "It is over, but we're just beginning," he murmured.

She smiled against his lips, laughing as he picked her up and carried her to the bedroom, not letting anything get in their way.

Epilogue

Three months later

LACEY SLIPPED HER FOOT out of her sandal and slid the pads of her bare toes along the length of his calf, her subtle flirting hidden under the table. When Jarod coughed abruptly as her foot flirted higher up his thigh, sneaking inside the loose material of his shorts, she laughed and enjoyed the mix of playful censure and desire in his eyes.

"You're bad, you know that?" he said. "I could have scalded myself on that slice of pizza, or dumped my beer down the front of my clothes, and then what would we have done?"

"I guess we'd have to go somewhere and get those clothes off, or I'd have to kiss it and make it better," she said, not the least bit repentant. In fact, her making him dump that beer was sounding like a good idea. It was a perfectly sunny, seventy-degree December day in Texas, but suddenly she was feeling a bit overheated.

"Hey, you two, this is a public area. Stop before I have to make up some new version of the fire code," Ryan Murphy joked, holding out a chair for Jackie as they arrived.

"This is great. Wearing summer clothes in winter. I may have to move here," Jackie commented, stretching bare arms above her head. Ryan caught one and kissed it, making her blush.

"And leave the best city in the world?" Ryan said in his heavy Brooklyn accent.

"Maybe. Maybe not," Jackie flirted. Her friend seemed happier and more herself than Lacey had seen her be in a while. Ryan was a good man, and exactly what Jackie deserved.

Lacey smiled at them, happy to be here, basking in the sun, the company, and the free time she was enjoying at the end of a very busy several months. Jackie lifted the beer that the waitress delivered to their riverside table, as people walked by the restaurant's patio.

"To the end of a successful project, and to our fearless leader for making it all come together in the end," she said, focusing on Lacey, making it her turn to blush.

"Hey, I could never have done it without you, Jackie, not to mention twelve sexy, barely clothed men," she joked, though she was only interested in one of the dozen, and he knew it. Things were good.

"To barely clothed men, then," Jackie repeated gustily, but only hers and Lacey's bottles met. Ryan and Jarod both put their beers down, comically refusing to join that particular toast.

"This was a fabulous idea, though, Jarod. A minivacation for all of us," Lacey added.

"I never spent much time in San Antonio…but we'll be changing that," he said, his foot finding its way over to nudge at Lacey's. "My transfer went through," he announced, and a hail of cheers went up.

Lacey was happiest of all. Three months of traveling back and forth from New York to El Paso were at an end. She could move to San Antonio, and she was sure she could find work in Texas, especially with the recommendations and exposure *Bliss* had offered her.

"Hey. Wait. I thought the only position open in San Antonio was the captain's?"

"That's right," he said calmly, leaning back in his chair. He looked at her from underneath that hat, those gorgeous brown eyes telegraphing her all kinds of wicked messages.

"But you didn't want to be captain. You wanted to be out in the field."

"Um, honey," Ryan spoke up, "why don't we go take a look at the river for a moment, until the food gets here? When we go home, all there will be is snow and slush," he said tactfully, taking Jackie's hand as they left the table.

"Jarod, I don't want you taking a job you'll be miserable in just to be near me."

As much as she wanted to be with him, he'd never asked her to give up her career, and she couldn't ask the same of him.

"Happy means being near you, in case you haven't noticed. Spending days on the road, tracking fugitives and drug-runners through the desert, has lost some of its charm, to say the least. I'll be busy in the new job, it'll be different, but I'll be coming home every night to you."

Convinced, she leaned in to kiss him. "I guess I can't argue with that," she said huskily. "No long-term assignments for me, either, at least, not in the near future."

"Speaking of long-term, there was something else I wanted to ask you about," he said, wrapping her hand in his.

"What's that?"

Reaching into his pocket with his other hand, he pulled out a small blue box. Tiffany's. Oh, my.

Oh, my, oh, my, oh, my, was all she could think, as he released her hand to open the box to reveal a glittering platinum-set diamond.

"I know it's only been a few months, and there's no rush, you can take your time, but—"

"Yes! Are you kidding me? Absolutely yes!" She jumped up, nearly overturning the table as she threw herself into his arms. She branded him with a long, scorching kiss that only broke when they drew applause. He looked deep into her eyes.

"I'll always be there for you. Always."

"I know. I'll be there for you, too," she promised, tears welling as he slipped the gorgeous ring on her left ring finger. "You really are a hero, Jarod."

"As long as you see me that way, that's all I care about, sweetheart."

Jackie and Ryan returned to the table, hooting, and congratulating them.

"Leave the table for a minute and see what happens," Ryan teased, slapping Jarod on the back and taking the seat he'd left earlier.

"Hmm, who knows who will be next?" Jarod quipped, watching Ryan's face, but he simply smiled, revealing nothing. The women were bent over the ring, sighing and talking animatedly, and Ryan shook his head.

"They might be at it for a while."

Jarod grinned, enjoying every second of it.

"Yeah, but that's okay. We have time."

* * * * *

*Celebrate 60 years of pure reading pleasure
with Harlequin!*

To commemorate the event, Harlequin Intrigue®
is thrilled to invite you to the wedding of The
Colby Agency's J. T. Baxley and his bride, Eve
Mattson.

That is, of course, if J.T. can find the woman who
left him at the altar. Considering he's a private
investigator for one of the top agencies in the
country—the best of the best—that shouldn't be
a problem. The real setback is that his bride isn't
who she appears to be…and her mysterious past
has put them both in danger.

*Enjoy an exclusive glimpse of Debra Webb's
latest addition to*
THE COLBY AGENCY:
ELITE RECONNAISSANCE DIVISION

THE BRIDE'S SECRETS

Available August 2009 from Harlequin Intrigue®.

The dark figures on the dock were still firing. The bullets cutting through the surface of the water without the warning boom of shots told Eve they were using silencers.

That was to her benefit. Silencers decreased the accuracy of every shot and lessened the range.

She grabbed for the rocks. Scrambled through the darkness. Bumped her knee on a boulder. Cursed.

Burrowing into the waist-deep grass, she kept low and crawled forward. Faster. Pushed harder. Needed as much distance as possible.

Shots pinged on the rocks.

J.T. scrambled alongside her.

He was breathing hard.

They had to stay close to the ground until they reached the next row of warehouses. Even though she was relatively certain they were out of range at this point, she wasn't taking any risks. And she wasn't slowing down.

J.T. had to keep up.

The splat of a bullet hitting the ground next to Eve had her rolling left. Maybe they weren't completely out of range.

She bumped J.T. He grunted.

His injured arm. Dammit. She could apologize later.

Half a dozen more yards.

Almost in the clear.

As she reached the cover of the alley between the first two warehouses she tensed.

Silence.

No pings or splats.

She glanced back at the dock. Deserted.

Time to run.

Her car was parked another block down.

Pushing to her feet, she sprinted forward. The wet bag dragged at her shoulder. She ignored it.

By the time she reached the lot where her car was parked, she had dug the keys from her pocket and hit the fob. Six seconds later she was behind the wheel. She hit the ignition as J.T. collapsed into the passenger seat. Tires squealed as she spun out of the slot.

"What the hell did you do to me?"

From the corner of her eye she watched him shake his head in an attempt to clear it.

He would be pissed when she told him about the tranquilizer.

She'd needed him cooperative until she formulated a plan. A drug-induced state of unconsciousness had been the fastest and most efficient method to ensure his continued solidarity.

"I can't really talk right now." Eve weaved into the right lane as the street widened to four lanes. What she needed was traffic. It was Saturday night—shouldn't be that difficult to find as soon as they were out of the old warehouse district.

A glance in the rearview mirror warned that their unwanted company had caught up.

Sensing her tension, J.T. turned to peer over his left shoulder.

"I hope you have a plan B."

She shot him a look. "There's always plan G." Then she pulled the Glock out of her waistband.

Cutting the steering wheel left, she slid between two vehicles. Another veer to the right and she'd put several cars between hers and the enemy.

She was betting they wouldn't pull out the firepower in the open like this, but a girl could never be too sure when it came to an unknown enemy.

Deep blending was the way to go.

Two traffic lights ahead the marquis of a movie theater provided exactly the opportunity she was looking for.

The digital numbers on the dash indicated it was just past midnight. Perfect timing. The late movie would be purging its audience into the crowd of teenagers who liked hanging out in the parking lot.

She took a hard right onto the property that sported a twelve-screen theater, numerous fast-food hot spots and a chain superstore. Speeding across the lot, she selected a lane of parking slots. Pulling in as close to the theater entrance as possible, she shut off the engine and reached for her door.

"Let's go."

Thankfully he didn't argue.

Rounding the hood of her car, she shoved the Glock into her bag, then wrapped her arm around J.T.'s and merged into the crowd.

With her free hand she finger-combed her long hair. It was soaked, as were her clothes. The kids she bumped into noticed, gave her death-ray glares.

They just didn't know.

As she and J.T. moved in closer to the building, she grabbed a baseball cap from an innocent bystander. The crowd made it easy. The kid who owned the cap had made it even easier by stuffing the cap bill-first into his waistband at the small of his back.

Pushing through the loitering crowd, she made her way to the side of the building next to the main entrance. She pushed J.T. against the wall and dropped her bag to the ground. Peeled off her tee and let it fall.

His gaze instantly zeroed in on her breasts, where the cami she wore had glued to her skin like an extra layer. A zing of desire shot through her veins.

Not the time.

With a flick of her wrist she twisted her hair up and clamped the cap atop the blond mass.

"They're coming," J.T. muttered as he gazed at some point beyond her.

"Yeah, I know." She planted her palms against the wall on either side of him and leaned in. "Keep your eyes open. Let me know when they're inside."

Then she planted her lips on his.

* * * * *

Will J.T. and Eve be caught in the moment?
Or will Eve get the chance to
reveal all of her secrets?
Find out in
THE BRIDE'S SECRETS
by Debra Webb
Available August 2009 from Harlequin Intrigue®

We'll be spotlighting a different series every month throughout 2009 to celebrate our 60th anniversary.

LOOK FOR
HARLEQUIN INTRIGUE®
IN AUGUST!

To commemorate the event, Harlequin Intrigue® is thrilled to invite you to the wedding of the Colby Agency's J.T. Baxley and his bride, Eve Mattson.

Look for *Colby Agency: Elite Reconnaissance*

THE BRIDE'S SECRETS
BY DEBRA WEBB

Available August 2009

www.eHarlequin.com

You're invited to join our Tell Harlequin Reader Panel!

By joining our new reader panel you will:

- Receive Harlequin® books—they are FREE and yours to keep with no obligation to purchase anything!
- Participate in fun online surveys
- Exchange opinions and ideas with women just like you
- Have a say in our new book ideas and help us publish the best in women's fiction

In addition, you will have a chance to win great prizes and receive special gifts!
See Web site for details. Some conditions apply.
Space is limited.

To join, visit us at
www.TellHarlequin.com.

REQUEST YOUR FREE BOOKS!

2 FREE NOVELS PLUS 2 FREE GIFTS!

HARLEQUIN®

Blaze™

Red-hot reads!

HB09R3

COMING NEXT MONTH
Available July 28, 2009

#483 UNBRIDLED Tori Carrington
After being arrested for a crime he didn't commit, former Marine Carter Southard is staying far away from the one thing that's always gotten him into trouble—women! Unfortunately, his sexy new attorney, Laney Cartwright, is making that very difficult....

#484 THE PERSONAL TOUCH Lori Borrill
Professional matchmaker Margot Roth needs to give her latest client the personal touch—property mogul Clint Hilton is a playboy extraordinaire and is looking for a date...for his mother. But while Margot's setting up mom, Clint decides Margot's for him. Let the seduction begin!

#485 HOT UNDER PRESSURE Kathleen O'Reilly
Where You Least Expect It
Ashley Larsen and David McLean are hot for each other. Who knew the airport would be the perfect place to find the perfect sexual partner? But can the lust last when it's a transcontinental journey every time these two want to hook up?

#486 SLIDING INTO HOME Joanne Rock
Encounters
Take me out to the ball game... Four sexy major leaguers are duking it out for the ultimate prize—the Golden Glove award. Little do they guess that the women fate puts in their path will offer them even more of a challenge...and a much more satisfying reward!

#487 STORM WATCH Jill Shalvis
Uniformly Hot!
During his stint in the National Guard, Jason Mauer had seen his share of natural disasters. But when he finds himself in a flash flood with an old crush—sexy Lizzy Mann—the waves of desire turn out to be too much....

#488 THE MIGHTY QUINNS: CALLUM Kate Hoffmann
Quinns Down Under
Gemma Moynihan's sexy Irish eyes are smiling on Callum Quinn! Charming the ladies has never been quiet Cal's style. But he plans to charm the pants off luscious Gemma—until he finds out she's keeping a dangerous secret...

www.eHarlequin.com

HBCNMBPA0709